BLOOD FOR BLOOD

"He got in a row with my partner, ma'am," Hamp said.

She ripped her face around and glared at him. "I am not ma'am. My name is Kathren."

"Yes, ma'am. I mean Kathren." He took off his hat for her.

"Did this happen on our property?"

"I guess so. It happened at the tank. Ten miles south of here."

"Then it's murder."

"Kathren, Texas law won't see it that way. They both were armed and got into it."

"I'll go see the sheriff and swear out a warrant for whoever did it."

"Kathren, this is your husband. Do you want him buried?" Shocked by the impression that all this woman wanted was some kind of revenge, he couldn't believe her reaction. No tears, no emotion. Only anger.

"I certainly don't want you to bury him." Her cold look would have frozen a peach orchard.

"Can I put the body somewhere for you?"

"Hell, no!" she screamed in his face. "I'll see you in hell for doing this. Do you hear me?"

Ralph Compton

Trail to
Fort Smith

A Ralph Compton Novel
By Dusty Richards

A SIGNET BOOK

SIGNET
Published by New American Library, a division of
Penguin Group (USA) Inc., 375 Hudson Street,
New York, New York 10014, U.S.A.
Penguin Books Ltd, 80 Strand,
London WC2R 0RL, England
Penguin Books Australia Ltd, 250 Camberwell Road,
Camberwell, Victoria 3124, Australia
Penguin Books Canada Ltd, 10 Alcorn Avenue,
Toronto, Ontario, Canada M4V 3B2
Penguin Books (N.Z.) Ltd, Cnr Rosedale and Airborne Roads,
Albany, Auckland 1310, New Zealand

Penguin Books Ltd, Registered Offices:
80 Strand, London WC2R 0RL, England

First published by Signet, an imprint of New American Library,
a division of Penguin Group (USA) Inc.

First Printing, April 2004
10 9 8 7 6 5 4 3 2 1

THE IMMORTAL COWBOY

This is respectfully dedicated to the "American Cowboy." His was the saga sparked by the turmoil that followed the Civil War, and the passing of more than a century has by no means diminished the flame.

True, the old days and the old ways are but treasured memories, and the old trails have grown dim with the ravages of time, but the spirit of the cowboy lives on.

In my travels—to Texas, Oklahoma, Kansas, Nebraska, Colorado, Wyoming, New Mexico, and Arizona—I always find something that reminds me of the Old West. While I am walking these plains and mountains for the first time, there is this feeling that a part of me is eternal, that I have known these old trails before. I believe it is the undying spirit of the frontier calling, allowing me, through the mind's eye, to step back into time. What is the appeal of the Old West of the American frontier?

It has been epitomized by some as the dark and bloody period in American history. Its heroes—Crockett, Bowie, Hickok, Earp—have been reviled and criticized. Yet the Old West lives on, larger than life.

It has become a symbol of freedom, when there was always another mountain to climb and another river to cross; when a dispute between two men was settled not with expensive lawyers, but with fists, knives or guns. Barbaric? Maybe. But some things never change. When the cowboy rode into the pages of American history, he left behind a legacy that lives within the hearts of us all.

—*Ralph Compton*

The Trail to Fort Smith

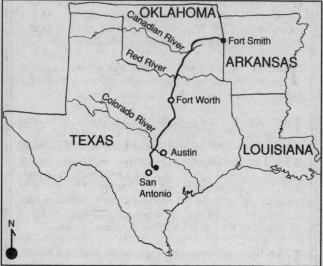

Prologue

"You're a lying, cheating, double-dealing card shark!" Clint used both hands to throw the table over in the gambler's face. Then his right hand shot in a flash to the butt of his .44. The boiling gunsmoke from the gambler's derringer going off and the ear-shattering blasts of the Colt in Clint's right fist caused Hamp to jump up to the aid of his partner. The lights went out. In a high-pitched, hysterical tone, a whore began screaming. A thick fog of spent gunsmoke veiled the saloon's dark interior. In all the confusion, Hamp caught Clint's gartered sleeve to pull him out of the melee.

"Time to lay tracks, hoss," Hamp said, so his partner knew who it was had ahold of his gun arm.

"My money . . ."

"Right now, it's your life." He pulled harder.

"That guy you just shot lives here. We ain't nothing but some itinerant drovers."

They forced their way through the milling crowd, out the front entrance, and onto the porch in the confusion and panic of the working girls and the shouting customers. Once outside, Hamp drew a breath of fresh night air. They nodded at each other, ducked under the hitch rail, took their reins and mounted.

"Up that hill," Hamp said, and they tore off.

Half a block from the saloon, their horses running wide open, a figure stepped out into the dark street to block their path. The silhouette tried to draw a weapon from his shoulder holster.

"Halt!" That was all he managed. Clint's boot caught him in the chest, which caused Clint's racing horse to shy hard against Hamp's mount. The collision with Clint's boot sent the town law flying into the side of a wagon. Hamp dared look back over his shoulder for a second to see the stricken lawman wilting to the ground in the darkness. Better than shooting him, anyway. He lashed his horse around the corner and up the steep street after his fast-disappearing partner.

Their lathered ponies were spent when they reached the top of the long hill. Halted to let them catch their breath, Hamp looked down at the dark snake of the Arkansas River circling around far-off Fort Smith and the twinkling lights of Van Buren underneath them. Time that they were G.T.T. Gone to Texas. No sign of any pursuit, they set out toward the northwest on wagon tracks to swing back through the Indian Nation and take the Texas–Fort Smith Trail home.

"He had cards up his sleeve. You saw that ace fall out," Clint said as they trotted down the dirt road. He sounded like he was talking more to himself than to his partner. Hamp had seen the card spill out of the gambler's sleeve the same moment Clint did and knew exactly what would happen next in those precious seconds before all hell broke loose.

"We need to push west," Hamp said. Once in the Indian Nation, Arkansas law couldn't touch them. At the moment, it was the most important thing he could think about—getting away from any of Arkansas law's jurisdiction.

"What're we going this way for?"

"So they can't arrest you."

"Aw, hell, they ain't going to run us down over killing no card shark that had it coming. Not like he wasn't armed. He had a derringer."

"Clint, you don't know, he may be a powerful man in that town."

"Sure. Let's ride. But you see a place we can get us something to eat, let's stop anyway. I'm starved."

"Over in the Nation."

Two hours later they came down the grade off a mountain and saw a downstairs light on in a two-story business.

"How late you reckon it is?" Clint asked.

"Must be close to midnight."

"Maybe we can get some food here. Looks like a store or saloon of some sort. I ain't ate anything since breakfast." He rubbed his flat belly.

Hamp twisted in the saddle and looked back in the starry night at the inky-dark hardwood-clad slope. Nothing he could see or hear, except some foxhounds running off into the night. Maybe they could afford to take some time and eat. No telling where they'd find anything else in this backcountry before daylight.

They dismounted at the hitch rail and Hamp made certain his gun was loose in his holster when he followed his burly pard up the steps. The front door was open. In the flickering candlelight he could see a bar on one side and store goods on shelves to the left.

"Well, howdy," a short, older man with bushy whiskers said from behind the bar.

"We in the Nation?" Clint asked.

"Nope, but you're close. You can't buy whiskey over there." He slammed a bottle down on the bar to show his evidence.

"We're close." Clint turned to see if that satisfied his partner.

"How close?" Hamp asked, looking around the place.

"Half a mile. That's why I'm right here. You get thirsty over there, you can ride over here." The man set two shot glasses on the bar. "First shot's on the house. My name's McGillacartie." After he put the bottle down again, he took a hickory stick and began to pound it on the ceiling.

"What the hell is that for?" Clint demanded with a suspicious scowl.

"Wake up my girls. Oh, they'd be mad if they knowed I had some real cowboys down here and never woke them."

"How old are your girls?" Clint asked, raising the jigger to toss it down.

The old man gave him a devilish wink. "Old enough to butcher, if you know what I mean."

"We were looking for some food," Hamp said, not wanting to get into some family deal with this guy's daughters.

The whiskey tossed down, Clint nodded at the owner. "Good stuff."

At the shrill sound of women's voices, they both turned to see a flurry of high-held skirts and petticoats exposing shapely legs prancing down the staircase.

"Oh, Paw, who's here?" the front one asked, stopping halfway down so the obviously taller one colliding into her. They were not teens. They were at least in their twenties, Hamp decided. Both had long noses and limp brown hair, but Hamp had seen worse. He knew Clint had too.

"These gents are hungry, girls."

"Fur what, Paw?"

"I think food first is what these gents wants."

Clint nodded and in his usual bold fashion said, "I'm Clint Barton and this is my pard, Hamp Moser."

"Nice to meet you," the short one said, and they both curtsied for them at the foot of the stairs.

"I'm Raenita May and this is my sister, Delphia June. We'll go whup you boys up some vittles. You drink some of Paw's fine whiskey and get real comfortable." Raenita May came prancing over and ran her finger under Clint's chin and smiled big at him. "I think we're going to have a real fun time after we feed you, huh, Delphia June?"

The tall one barely smiled, but nodded real quick in agreement.

"Delphia June is a little bashful," Raenita May said, turning to Hamp. "But she's nice and tall and just your type." She drove her fist playfully into his muscle-corded belly. "You'll see." Then she waved for her sister to follow her and they went skipping into the rear kitchen.

Clint ordered another shot. Still concerned about pursuit by the Van Buren officials, Hamp went out on the porch and listened in the night. Just bugs buzzing and a few dogs off somewhere barking. He'd be grateful when they were over the Indian Nation line. At times he couldn't impress enough on his partner the urgency of something important—like moving on.

McGillacartie came to the door. "You want to put them horses in the barn out back. I'll get you a light. Water in the tank and there's some grain in the barrel if'n you want to feed 'em."

"I think I'll do that." Hamp stuck his head in the front door to tell Clint his intentions. "I'm going to water the horses and feed them. We still got a long ways to ride."

"Sure, pard," Clint said, busy talking to Raenita May.

Paw brought him a lamp and Hamp took the horses around to the old log shed with tie stalls.

After letting them have their fill of water from the spring-fed tank, he loosened the cinches but decided against unsaddling them. They'd need to ride on in a short while and get over in the Nation. At last the two ponies were tied in a stall, side by side. With the lamp, he went looking for feed. The grain he found in the barrel was old flint corn, but he poured a scoopful in each feed box for the cow ponies. Beat nothing, and the hay was old and moldy so he ignored it and, at last satisfied that they were cared for, he headed back. Before he walked around to the front, he could hear someone sawing on a fiddle.

When he arrived at the porch and could see in the doorway, he saw Clint and the short sister dancing a jig. If anyone else was there, those two would never have known it. They polkaed around that room and her dress was flying. Hamp turned his ear to listen again for any sounds of a posse, but he couldn't hear much for the music and the loud-shouting dancers. They sure were having themselves a party. Eaten up with wanting for him and his pard to get the hell out of there, Hamp took a seat at a side table.

Delphia June came out of the kitchen and sat in a chair beside him. "They're sure having a big time, ain't they?"

"You dance?"

She pursed her thin lips and shook her head. "I never learned how."

Hamp nodded, grateful. He didn't feel like dancing anyway. Wasn't drunk enough, he guessed.

"Want some more whiskey?" she asked with her chin down and her long, bony hands clasped in her lap.

"No."

"That's okay, you don't have to drink, if'n you don't want to."

"I don't want to," Hamp said. "I mean, I don't want any whiskey right now."

"Right now, you mean?" She nodded sharply. "I don't even like it."

"Food cooking?" he asked, smelling something.

"Yes. It'll be ready pretty soon. Heating it in the oven. Stove was still hot."

"Let's go see about it."

"Oh, you want to see about it?"

"Yes." He rose and looked at her to join him.

She shrugged and nodded. "We can go see about it."

"Fine. I'm getting antsy sitting here."

She squinted her eyes at him. "Is that like having 'em in your pants?"

"Almost."

"I sat down on an anthill once and never knowed it. When I figured it out they was all over me. I got so scared I run and I run."

"You get rid of them?" He smiled to himself. He must have got the duller sister. The other one was shouting and jigging away around the room with Clint to the old man's fiddle music.

"Yeah, but I could still feel them for days afterwards crawling around down there. Oh." Her shoulders trembled under the dress material. "You know what I mean?"

"I think so," he said, leaning his shoulder against the kitchen door facing.

She bent over, opened the oven door and peeked in. "About hot. I better make some gravy. My gravy ain't never as good as her'n. But she's too busy."

"Yeah," Hamp said, looking back at his partner downing another quick whiskey with sweat streaming down his face, ready to dance another jig with Raenita May.

Delphia June began browning flour in a skillet on the stove top. She was singing "Turkey in the Straw" to the music and had a nice voice. He took off his high crown hat and rested the back of his head on the hand-hewn door facing.

"Get much business here?" he asked.

"Lots of Indians come over here when they get their allotments. We have to stock up for that time. Boy"—she looked hard at her skillet contents—"I don't know how much we sell then."

"Guess you got regular customers come by."

"Sometimes, whenever they sell something like a hawg or a good hunting dawg." She looked up and her blue eyes questioned him. "You got a girl back home?"

"No, why?"

"I just wondered if you were taken." She idly stirred the browning flour.

"No." He laughed aloud. "I'm not taken. Does that matter?"

She shrugged her shoulders slow like to dismiss his concern. "I use to have dreams." She stopped, poured the milk in and began mixing it. "Don't be lumpy," she said to the gravy and used her wooden spoon furiously on it.

"What were your dreams about?"

"Oh, that a nice cowboy would come by here someday and say, 'Delphia June, go with me.'" She looked so dreamily pleased with the notion, he could've sworn she had stars in her eyes.

"But he never came?"

"No, but this gravy ain't lumpy." Pleased acting, she ladled spoonfuls up and let them run back into the white mixture. "You did bring me some good luck, anyway."

They all ate the roast pork, potatoes and Delphia June's gravy that Raenita May said she could have made thicker and it would have been better. After the meal, Hamp's partner, Clint, and the shorter sister went charging upstairs. The old man put up his fiddle and disappeared. He left Hamp and Delphia June sitting at the table with a flickering candle.

After a few minutes, Hamp could hear the loud creaking of a protesting rope bed upstairs. Delphia June put her folded hands on top of the table, swallowed real hard. "I know I ain't as good as her, but if'n you'd want to . . ."

He reached over and patted her on the arm. "You're better than her. But not tonight. Not cause you ain't—I mean, nothing's wrong with you. My mind's on Texas and when my pard comes down them stairs in a little while we're heading for home."

"You're a good man, Hamp Moser. I won't never forget you." She raised up, bent over and kissed him on the forehead. Then she went quietly upstairs.

No telling when Clint would get his business over. Hamp stuck his dusty boots across to another chair and dozed. When he awoke, the candle was about burned down. He felt the pressing urge to go outside and vent his bladder. Still half asleep, he leaned back in the chair and studied the light dancing on the ceiling. He could hear Clint's loud snoring upstairs. His partner was up there sleeping it off.

He went out through the kitchen, down the steps and was about to pee under the star-flecked sky when he heard voices with a drawl talking in whispers.

"Their hosses're in the barn."

"Good. Two of you take the back door. Station two men at each door and window and shoot to kill 'em if they try to come out. This damn pair of Texans are sure enough deadly killers. Shoot first and ask questions later."

"I hear you, Toby. Let 'em have it."

Hamp fled to the cover of a small empty chicken coop, knocked off his cowboy hat, caught it and crouched low to get inside the coop. Nothing he could do against twenty or thirty armed men. Just so they didn't shoot Clint or he didn't try something suicidal like attempting to shoot his way out. Filled with dread over the outcome, Hamp watched in the shadowy light as the armed men took command of the back door and two of them with guns drawn went creeping inside the kitchen. He felt for his

Colt—five shots and he'd be through. A warning from him might get Clint up, but it would also be liable to get him killed as well. Damned if you do and damned if you don't. They were sure outnumbered and outgunned.

Next he heard Raenita May screaming her head off and Clint cursing away. Hamp could make out the sounds of the commotion going on upstairs from where he was squatted down in the small, stinking coop. But when the posse found only one Texan in the building, the armed members ran all over the place looking for him. Twice they stopped a few feet from his position and came close to looking in the coop. He had the Colt ready to blast them if they tried.

Since they made no threat to lynch his partner, he felt better hid out in the foul-smelling brooder. In a while they gave up their search for him and talked about taking their prisoner back to jail in Van Buren.

"We can look for the other one tomorrow," the leader said.

Not daring to leave his shelter right away, in case it was a trick, Hamp remained inside. The cramps in his leg from squatting so long forced him to at last sit in the dried litter and try to work out the aches as quietly as possible.

With the dawn, Delphia June came and sat in

the back doorway with her elbows on her knees, holding a towel and crying in her hands. Her obvious concern touched him, but he still was uncertain that they hadn't left some posse members about the place. After a while Raenita May and McGillacartie began having a shouting match about who'd done what wrong, so he decided the coast was clear.

When Hamp started to wiggle his way out and Delphia June saw him, it was like he had lifted that girl's spirit to the heavens.

"You're alive!" she shrieked. In an instant, she bolted over to him and began hugging and kissing him. Paw and the other sister rushed out there, and started beating him on the back.

"How did you do it? How did you do it?"

"I don't know. Blind luck, I guess. But how do I get my pard out of that jail?"

Paw held his hands up and silenced all the girls' questions. "You two go in the house and let me and Mr. Moser here talk. We've got business. Serious business to discuss."

When they were alone, Paw said, "You serious about getting him out?" The man's blue eyes narrowed and he looked hard at Hamp.

He stared back at the old man. He wanted his pard outside and headed for home with him.

"Yes. Sure as I'm astanding here. I'm dead serious about getting him out."

"It's going to cost you. Ain't like he spit on the sidewalk."

"I can raise some money. Don't have much on me, but I can get it if we've got a good chance to get him out. How much will it cost?"

"A thousand."

"Whew. A thousand?" The amount pained him, but he knew getting Clint out of the Van Buren jail would be no small undertaking.

Paw's head bobbed. "I think we can do it for that."

"How? Bribe the guards?"

"Yes, I think it can be arranged for them to turn their backs. Plus have some fresh horses in relays to get him out of Arkansas. But I want one more thing if I do all this for you. You know it'll be real dangerous for me to arrange and do all this for you and him?"

"Sure. How much do you want?"

"Don't want any money." McGillacartie shook his head. "I want you to marry my Delphia June."

"Marry her!" Hamp felt the blood draining from his face. A large constriction formed in his throat and cut off his air.

Paw spat tobacco to the side. "She ain't cut

out for this business. Lord love her. She ain't daft. And she ain't ugly. But she's never had a real boyfriend. You're the first. The very first guy ever treated her nice. Now Raenita May can get along fine on her own, but I ain't getting any younger. Something happens to me, Raenita could run this place and survive.

"I wants to see them girls happy is all I want."

Hamp looked hard at the emerald hillside of tall oak trees and gathered ideas in his mind about this jail business. "I think I can get some Texas drovers from over around Fort Smith and we can bust open that jail."

"I bet you can. But who's going to die if you try it? Your partner, Clint? He'll sure be in the line of fire."

Hamp shook his head, unable to think of anything else, least of all about him taking a wife as being his partner's only salvation. "I better have some whiskey."

Chapter 1

Hamp paced the floor of the McGillacartie combination store and bar. As Raenita Mae worked the broom to remove the grit from the surface of the worn boards, she paused to look up at him.

"Paw'll be back with your pard in a few hours. He knows his business."

When Hamp didn't answer her, she glared at him with an "oh-what-the-hell" look. Then she went back to her sweeping. "You'd think Delphia June was some kind of innocent thing up there, all dressed up like—well, you'll see." Her efforts at sweeping began to make small piles of dirt across the room. "She ought to be down here working instead of getting ready to marry you. How long you think that'll last?"

"Last?" He shook his head, not entirely certain of Raenita Mae's meaning. "I guess the rest of our life." In his current state of concern for his pard's welfare, he'd thought little about his promise to take on a mate. Why wouldn't the two of them stay together? That's what married people did where he came from—stayed married. Raenita May had mean ways of belittling her younger sister, whether it was saying her gravy was too thin or she had some lack of brains. In the three days that he'd been staying at their place, he found the older sister took satisfaction in putting Delphia June down, with either a subtle slight or openly sarcastic comments about Delphia June's well-intended actions.

Hamp walked to the open front door and stared out into the night, listening to the sizzling bugs in the trees. He'd be grateful when this was all over and they were on their way back to Texas. The thousand dollars he'd given the old man for Clint's delivery could be recovered in a good drive up there. He felt grateful to the drovers he'd found in the region who helped him make up the balance of the money he needed to reach that amount.

Most of them Texans wanted to storm the Van Buren jail, but Hamp knew that would endanger Clint's life, plus none of them needed to lose their lives if McGillacartie's plan worked. This wasn't the war, though many of them had fought in this region during the conflict. North of there a hundred miles, during the Elkhorn Tavern fight, Hamp had been with Texas cavalry when General James McCollough was shot down by a sniper.

He turned his ear to listen. There were sounds of horses coming and his hand shot to his hip. Standing aside from the door, he waved Rita Mae's back with his arm in case of trouble.

"Hamp? Hamp?"

The sound of his partner's voice drew a great feeling of relief over his entire body and he hurried outside to see the hatless Clint drop off his hard-breathing horse.

"Damn, you're a sight for sore eyes," Hamp said from the top of the porch.

"You too." They hugged each other in relief.

Paw dismounted. "Clint, go get that fresh horse out of the barn and you can meet the newlyweds down in the Nation. No telling when the law'll get on your trail."

"I'll head out," Hamp said.

"We'll hook up the wagon and team too, then," Paw said and spat tobacco to the side as they led the horses to the pens.

"How did it go?" Hamp asked

"Good. They left the cell open like Paw said they would and I walked out. Scared to death it was a trap and I'd get shot in the back out in the alley," Clint said, shaking his head in the starlight.

"I even saved you five hundred," Paw said and handed him the handful of money. "They was cheaper than I figured they'd be. You'll need it with a new wife and all."

"Thanks," Hamp said, not expecting the windfall savings, but he felt pleased to jam the refund inside his shirt. He'd be able to pay back all that he'd borrowed with it.

At the barn they switched Clint's saddle to his fresh horse.

"I'll meet you at Poteau River Crossing in two days," Clint said.

"We'll be there."

Clint hesitated and looked hard at his partner in the dim light. "You know you don't have to marry her?"

"I never in my life gone back on my word and I ain't starting now."

With his calloused hand, Clint clapped him on the shoulder. "You're a helluva partner. See you at the crossing."

"Yes."

Clint swung into the saddle and with a wave disappeared in the inky night. Somewhere off in the hardwood-cloaked hills an owl hooted. Its deep voice carried and then echoed with an eeriness that grabbed at Hamp's guts. He still had his part of the deal left to do. At least Clint was safe and headed for home.

"Best get this team hitched. You know why I chose you?" Paw said, breaking into Hamp's thoughts.

"We better get to cutting. No, why me?"

"Cause'n you got that way about you. You're the kind of guy'd never leave anyone in a lurch, least of all my daughter. Let's get them hosses hitched. There's a Cherokee preacher over in the Nation we can wake up about dawn and he can marry you two. Then you all can be on your way."

Midmorning, he shared the wagon seat with his new bride. They were coming off a steep grade and he could see glimpses of the grassy bottoms far below every once in a while through the post oak. She'd not said much since he kissed her in the preacher's parlor after the brief ceremony. Her sobbing sister clung to her, crying the whole time like they'd never see each other again and telling her to write every week.

"I've been thinking," he said, slapping the horses over a big root that grew across the road, "that I'd rename you, now you're my wife."

"You did, Mr. Moser. What will you call me?"

"I mean I'm going to shorten your first name to Junie."

Almost thrown off the seat by the rocking of the wagon over the hump, she grasped his arm. "Hamp, that would be just lovely."

He nodded and swung the horses around a big rock outcropping jutting up in the unimproved road. This whole situation of his marriage felt strange to him. He sure enough had a wife and they were into the first day of their life together and he knew as much about women as he did about the stars. No, he knew more about the stars, cause he could tell time by the Big Dipper and he couldn't tell nothing about her. Except she smelled good and he had this visceral feeling there would be lots more to this than a quick toss in the hay with some dove.

"You sure didn't get no bargain," she mumbled.

He reined in the team, locked the brake, tied off the reins and then used the side of his hand to lift her chin.

"Whatever we did before don't count. This is our day and it is the first one. We're shedding all that was behind us. From here on it's us and what we do. We're obligated to each other now."

She managed to nod as her eyes filled with

tears. "I won't ever do nothing to embarrass you, Hamp Moser. I promise."

"I won't either." He bear-hugged her and felt a great relief flow out of him. Damn, she felt so slight in his arms. And she was his wife.

Chapter 2

Heat waves distorted the drought-ridden country any way Hamp looked. A veil of dust from the cattle's cloven hooves filled the air. A bandanna over his mouth to breath through, Hamp swung his rope, blistering the tail-enders at the back of the herd that were unwilling to keep up the pace. Cattle bawling and the knock of one long horn whacking on another were all part of the sounds in his ears. Saddle leather creaked and his cow pony snorted the acrid powder from his nose, all sounds that ran into the dulling of Hamp Moser's mind.

Three days and they'd have this bunch of new stock back to the ranch. Besides the special comfort that being home in the hill country always afforded him, he'd have Junie to tend to him. In the past year since their marriage, his bride had become a real important fixture in his life. First thing he did was shorten her name on the hillside over the river. She never cared, kinda like he could say the moon was yellow and she'd go along with it. The intimate part of their marriage was more than he expected, but he'd had no idea that having such a hardworking female in his life could be so rewarding and make such a difference.

Junie kept a milk cow he'd bought for her. She made butter. Had her own chickens—why, he could go on for hours about his wife's bountiful garden and a cellar full of foodstuff. Back to work, he jobbed the pony with a spur to get in close and slapped the lagging small black steer with his lariat. Damn that slowpoke. He needed to keep up.

Through the brown curtain, he saw the youthful Miguel coming, standing in the stirrups looking for him.

He jerked down the mask. "What's wrong?"

"Clint, he wants you." The vaquero gave a head toss to the west side of the herd.

"Something gone wrong?"

Miguel's nod made him wonder.

"You keep them moving?" he said to the Mexican cowboy taking his place.

"Sí, señor."

He tied the coil of his lariat to the saddle, then

he booted the pony out of the dust. Riding at a short lope away from the herd through the leaf-less black mesquite, he wondered what was wrong. Where was Clint?

Then he saw his partner waving to him from a rise. He reined the pony around a bed of shriveled black pancake cactus and down into a wash. The bay gelding Daymus cat-hopped up the steepest slope and loped to the top.

He reined him up. "What's wrong?"

"They want ten cents a head to water these cattle at the ranch up ahead."

"That the same place we usually camp?" Hamp frowned. No charges the last time they came through there. Things must be getting tough for folks to go to charging for stock water.

"I think he's a new owner. I never seen this guy before."

"Guess we better pay it. These cattle ain't had anything to eat in a while and with a bellyful of water in them at least we might get most of them home alive."

Clint's pale blue eyes had taken on that hard look. Hamp recognized the growing fire in his partner. This look always occurred before his anger was about to override his good sense.

"This drought's got lots of folks on the brink," said Hamp. "All we've got to feed these critters at home is the dried-up cornfields we bought on the stalk."

"Yeah, but charging other ranchers for water—"

"Hey, these are tough times. I never ever seen so many dead cattle on the range, going down to Mexico or coming back."

"You say pay him?" Clint's disgusted scowl covered his unshaven face in the shade of his felt hat.

"I say pay him."

"Guess every outfit needs a thinker. Man, only you could have ever figured out how to get me out of that Arkansas jail."

"You still thinking on that?"

Hamp was watching the herd pass by. Even in the dust, he could see how he could hang his hat on these thin critters' hipbones. Cheap cattle out of Mexico—but they'd be expensive if very many died before they got them to some feed and free water.

"Let Miguel ride drag. You come with me," Clint said.

Hamp nodded and put Daymus in beside his partner's roan. Stirrup by stirrup, they headed north through the drought-scorched desert.

The tank was less than half full, Hamp discovered when they rode up on it. No cattle around. They scared off some birds and let their horses drink. Scooped out in a dry wash, someone had spent many man-hours building the tank with fresnoes and teams. But obviously the lack of rainfall and evaporation had taken a toll on the supply. Normally water covered several acres in this man-made basin.

"Notice he ain't had any cattle of his own down here," Hamp offered, checking the tracks and old droppings.

"'Reckon he's sold out?" Clint searched around, looking at the ground for signs.

Hamp shrugged. "No telling."

"Wouldn't be the first." Clint took off his hat and knelt down on the edge to wet his kerchief and mop his face. "Damn hot dry weather is sure holding on."

The whisker-faced cook for the outfit, a man in his fifties, Sam Hayes drove the chuck wagon up and halted his double team of mules short of the water's edge. Setting the brake and tying off the reins, he said, "I better fill my water barrel first, 'fore them cattle stir it up into mud soup."

The short man with a stiff-legged limp took the keg-size barrel off the rack on the side of the wagon and headed for the edge of the dingy water to fill it.

Hamp went after his other keg to help him.

They'd need all the water both barrels could hold.

"I ain't seen that Muldoone guy since we talked the first time I rode up here," Clint said. He looked off to the north for a sign of him.

"He'll no doubt be along to collect his money," Hamp assured him.

"I ain't doubting that."

"Just pay the man," Hamp said, hoisting the filled barrel on his shoulder and heading for the chuck wagon with it.

The remuda arrived. The loose horses came down the sloping sides to get a drink, snorting in the dust. Petey Sims, the young boy who wrangled them and helped Sam, rode over. "Big Joe is limping. Only started doing it a ways back."

"We'll cut him out," Clint said. "See what's ailing him. Thanks, Petey."

"Pretty watchful," Hamp said to his partner about the young wrangler.

"Good boy. Got good folks."

Hamp agreed and looked off to the north again. Dust. Must be Muldoone coming back to collect his fee. He hoped the man didn't rouse his partner's ire. Clint could get his back up in a hurry and it didn't take much of anything to ignite him.

Muldoone wore a thick mustache, had round eyeglasses, a floppy-brimmed hat. In his bat-wing chaps and gray vest he looked the part of a ramrod. Rode a big black stud horse and had a hard set to his eyes. Hamp saw right away he was the kind that could kindle trouble out of Clint in a minute. He considered the situation and felt concerned over the possible outcome, if Muldoone was as big a fool as he suspected him to be.

Should he go and make the deal or let Clint? His partner was the front man—better leave things like they were. From where he stood by the wagon he could see the two men confronting each other and he frowned. He could hear their voices getting louder, but couldn't make out the words. They were into it was all he knew. He started down the loose dirt in their direction to stop them. What was going on? They'd agreed to pay Muldoone. Simple enough.

Then he saw Clint's hand go for the Colt. The words froze in Hamp's mouth—*DON'T!* Both men shot at the same time and Clint's roan shied sideways. Muldoone was pitched off the back of his horse by the force of the bullet that struck him. Hamp could see that Clint was holding his arm.

Before Hamp could catch him, the stud that Muldoone rode left out, pitching and bucking, stirrups slapping his sides.

"Go catch that horse," he shouted at Petey.

The boy nodded that he had heard and ran for his mount. The loose sand was tough to run in, but Hamp caught the spooked roan's rein.

"You hit bad?" he asked.

"Naw, just a scratch." Clint's eyes looked hard as an angry wolf.

"We said we'd pay him. What the hell was the gunfight over?"

"Hell, he wanted a quarter apiece for them two damn water barrels we filled."

"Why in the hell didn't you just pay him?"

"That sumbitch—"

"Sam, check Clint out," Hamp said to the cook coming on the run. "I'll go see about Muldoone."

"I'll take care of him," said Sam, who also served as doctor for the outfit.

Hamp walked the twenty steps across the sand. Muldoone was on his back, not moving. The two bullet holes in his shirt oozed red blood from his chest. Hamp knelt beside him and felt his throat for his pulse. Nothing.

The man's brown eyes stared at the dust-covered round lenses of his eyeglasses. Hamp unhooked them from behind his ears, folded the frames and put them in the man's vest, then closed his eyes. Rising to his feet, he shook his head in disgust.

"A foolish damn deal."

When he got back to them, Sam had Clint's shirtsleeve torn open and blood was dripping off his fingers.

"I can stitch it. Not bad. Won't hurt him long. He'll live. What about the other jasper?" Sam asked, chewing hard on his jaw full of tobacco.

"He's gone."

Using Sam for a crutch, Clint cleared his throat and spat a hocker in the dust. "He hadn't been such a hothead he'd still be alive. Twenty-five cents a keg. Can't believe he'd try to hold a guy up for that."

"Which way is his ranch?" Hamp asked, searching around. They'd need to do something with the body.

"Damned if I know. He came from the north."

Clint nodded, seeing the boy Petey bringing back the stud horse.

"I'll take his body in."

"Tell 'em it was self defense," Clint said over his shoulder as Sam took him off to stitch his arm.

Hamp and the boy wrapped the body up in a

ground cloth and bound it with rope. Then they loaded it over the back of the snorty stud and tied it on good.

"Hold him, Petey." Hamp gave the boy the reins to the stallion, then went and found his own pony.

Stud horse in tow, Hamp rode around the tank at a trot. Despite a show of teeth, the stud led well and Hamp soon was on the ribbons of wagon tracks headed north. How far he would have to ride to find Muldoone's headquarters, he had no idea. The tracks looked fresh enough in the dust, so he decided to follow them.

Two hours later, he spotted a *jacal* and some sparse cottonwoods. The stud had come from there. He saw a Mexican woman hanging clothes look in his direction, and then seeing the load on the stud she put her hands to her mouth and came running. He guessed her to be in her early twenties.

"Oh, no, what happened to him?" she asked in a quavering voice, looking at the stallion and his load.

"He got in a gunfight. He your man?"

"Oh, no. He is the *patrón*." She paled at the words escaping her lips. With a wavering head shake, she backed away. "I-I only know who he is."

"Where did he live?"

"At the ranch—" She half stumbled, going backward toward the *jacal* like Hamp had the plague. "That way." She motioned to the north.

He nodded. The stud had been to this place only a short while before. He saw his fresh droppings on the ground at her hitch rack. He'd been hitched there for some time. Those apples obviously were from a well-fed animal, not a range one.

He turned the horses around and started back for the road. What was her name? He had never asked her. She acted so upset when he even mentioned any connection between them, it was obvious there must have been something going on. He suspected an affair of some sort between the two.

The western sky had turned copper red with sundown. Both horses were sweating from the heat and the hard pace he made them hold. The ranch was situated on a dried-up creek. A line of straggly cottonwoods snaked past it. He heard a dog bark and saw someone come out on the porch of the main house.

It was a woman. She wore pants and her hands were slid down in the front pockets. Thirty-five, perhaps. Her hair had some gray streaks and was pulled back severely enough to give her eyes a pinched look in the corners. She stood straight, and he saw right off that she bore a strong aura about herself.

She narrowed her lids, then ran off the porch to examine the wrapped body. He dismounted after checking around. No one else appeared to be there.

"How did this happen?" she demanded.

"He got in a row with my partner, ma'am."

She ripped her face around and glared at him. "I am not ma'am. My name is Kathren."

"Yes, ma'am. I mean Kathren." He took off his hat for her.

"Did this happen on our property?"

"I guess so. It happened at a tank. Ten miles south of here."

"Then it's murder."

"Kathren, Texas law won't see it that way. They both were armed and got into it."

"I'll go see the sheriff and swear out a warrant for whoever did it."

"Kathren, this is your husband. Do you want him buried?" Shocked by the impression that all this woman wanted was some kind of revenge, he couldn't believe her reaction. No tears, no emotion. Only anger.

"I certainly don't want you to bury him." Her cold look would have frozen a peach orchard.

"Can I put his body somewhere for you?"

"Hell, no!" she screamed in his face. In rage, she stepped forward, ripped the reins of the stud's bridle from his hand. "I'll see you in hell for doing this. Do you hear me?"

"Lady, is there anyone here on this ranch to help you?"

"None of your damn business. Get out of here!" She stomped her boot. "Go now!"

He stepped back and mounted his horse. Nothing he could do for her. My Gawd. He shook his head in dismay, lifted the reins high and turned his horse to leave.

"Get out of here!" she bellowed. "I'll see you hang for this! You bastard!"

He felt shaken. Short-loping his horse in the gray twilight across the vast featureless land, he headed back for camp. A sour deal from start to finish was all he could think about. He wished he had his Junie to hold and make it all go away.

Chapter 3

Clint rode ahead on the fifth day after the shooting incident to check on things. Hamp was determined to have the steers on feed by dark that night. The Ferguson farm where they had rented the forty acres of droughty corn to graze was the closest place. There were some water holes nearby in the about-dry creek on the place. Some springs were still flowing enough to fill them. The desert cattle would think they were in heaven in the coarse stalks. They'd soon fill up. Then they had some more burned-up crops to graze that had never made any ears before firing from the drought. In fact, Hamp felt certain they could make a very profitable fall drive to Fort Smith if they could get enough weight on the steers.

Cattle trader Erick Paulson had sent him a letter asking if they could bring a herd up with some flesh on them. He had some Indian beef contracts to fill. Hamp wrote him back for the details. Then they went to Mexico and bought this herd—knowing it would be a tough, dry trip back with weak cattle. Despite all the concern, they lost less than half a dozen head in the trip north.

They planned to graze the steers on the corn forage until they picked up some strength, then head them for the Nation. Word from drovers returning from Kansas said there was plenty of strong grass north of the Red River. A month in the fired corn and they'd start that way. They'd graze them up there in the Nation for sixty days and then head them north to meet Paulson's delivery dates.

Plenty of drovers that they knew took their herds to Kansas, but the two partners had found they could make more money easier by taking smaller bunches to specific markets like at Fort Smith, Arkansas. While a herd of two thousand would kill the smaller markets, seven hundred fleshy steers could make a good profit for them. That, and the fact that many drovers often got caught without any market at Abilene and had to stay over through the snowy winter in Kansas to even sell their herds, made Hamp pleased they could market theirs thirty days closer to home.

In the more familiar Texas hill country again, Hamp thought about being at his own place in another day. Some fluffy clouds, harbingers of monsoonal moisture, drifted in from the Gulf, bringing hope of needed rain to his mind. In another day he would be in his own bed with his wife, Junie, a thought that warmed him.

Three riders came from the south and approached the herd like they had business. Hamp watched them close like. They wore suits and at a distance they didn't look like troublemakers. He booted Jake, his big bay, in their direction. He reined up short of them and used the time to size them up.

"Howdy."

"This your herd?" the big man with the snowy mustache asked.

"Part. Name's Hamp Moser."

"Dave Colburn, sheriff in Madre County."

"Well, I'll let you know now that these cattle haven't been rustled."

"We've been tracking them from where a rancher was murdered."

Hamp eyed the other two. They appeared to be businessmen, hardly gun hands or even full-time lawmen. The small man looked like a clerk or store owner; he shrank in the saddle under Hamp's gaze. The third man had the pallor of a banker, someone the day's heat was burning up.

"You talking about Muldoone's death?" Hamp asked.

"Yes. Did you shoot him?" Colburn demanded.

"No. Secondly, if he had been murdered I'd never have taken his body to his wife. I offered to help her bury him."

"And hide the evidence."

"There were three witnesses," Hamp said.

"Who shot him?" Colburn's face looked drawn around his mouth and eyes.

"Muldoone went for his gun."

"Gawdamnit, if you didn't, then who shot him?"

"It isn't really important. It was self-defense."

"You damn drovers ain't coming in riding roughshod over the ranchers in my county." He pointed his finger like a gun at Hamp.

"We ain't in your county now. So why don't you turn that horse and ride back home. We came in peace. Muldoone was the unreasonable one."

"Yeah, that's what you say."

"No. That's what four of us will swear to."

Hamp saw the lawman sweep back his coat

and he knew what was coming next. Without a thought, except to take some swift action, he plunged his spurs into Jake's sides and the horse bolted forward. The bay's chest struck the sheriff at the knee and the force sent the lawman and his animal sprawling to the ground. Colburn's pistol flew out of his hand and the man cried out in pain. He was pinned down by his animal, his leg was being mauled underneath the struggling horse, which at last made it to its feet.

Hamp's right hand held his Colt on the two shocked men. "Don't try anything. You don't have any authority here. Except to die."

Both men raised their hands, looking upset at his poised gun and their moaning companion on the ground holding his leg. Obviously, neither man had the stomach for gunplay—or Colburn either, in his condition.

"You're a wanted man!" Colburn shouted. "I'll get you!"

"You aren't the law here."

"You'll find out what authority I have!"

"Better have him seen about," Hamp said to the two deputies. "I don't have time." He holstered his gun and took off after his disappearing herd.

This was a new turn of events. He knew he'd

better find his partner and also talk to Elliot Tanner, the Kerr-Mac County sheriff. Perhaps he'd overplayed his hand. Glancing back over his shoulder, he could see the two were trying to load Colburn on his horse. Hamp pushed Jake harder.

"Miguel, you boys water these cattle at the creek and put them in that corn that we bought from Hayes. One of you stay with the herd. I need to go find Clint."

"What happened back there?" The swarthy-faced youth frowned.

"Some gun-happy lawman tried to arrest me."

"What for?"

"Over that Muldoone shooting."

"What can I do?"

Hamp shook his head. "I'm headed for town and talking to a lawyer and Sheriff Tanner. I'll find Clint after that."

"I will tell Sam what you do and have Sancho stay with the herd tonight."

"Good. I'll be back tomorrow and we can discuss things."

"Sí. Be careful, señor. I would have come to help you."

"No, I handled it, right or wrong. It'll work

out," he said to reassure the concerned-looking young vaquero.

"Vaya con Dios."

"Same." Hamp turned Jake and headed out in a hard lope for Cedar Vale. Clint had promised to meet him at the Hayes place in the morning. No telling where he was rutting at—probably with the widow Nancy Turbow on Horse Creek. He'd better find Tanner first and figure out what to do next about Colburn.

Cedar Vale sat on the banks of the Rio Bueno, hardly more than a small creek except in times of flash floods. The place was just a cluster of *jacals* and weekend homes that the Germans used to stay in town for church before they went back to their far-flung ranches and farms. The business portion of the town clustered around the small stone courthouse in the square. Hamp left his sweaty horse at the rack and headed inside to find Tanner.

In the basement office, the forty-some-year-old lawman looked up behind a full mustache from the paperwork on his rolltop desk.

"Howdy, Hamp. You all just get back from Mexico?" The chair's springs creaked when he leaned back and swiveled it.

"Just rode in." The two shook hands.

"Have a seat. You look trail weary."

"I am. Let me start from the first—" Hamp began to tell him the Muldoone story. He went through to where he left the body with the widow and then told about his run-in with Colburn.

"Sounds like you did your part for the matter." Tanner leaned forward and nodded his head as if in consideration. "What was he going to arrest you for?"

"Murder, I guess. Damned if I know. But I do know it was an open-and-shut case of self-defense, and there are four of us to swear to that."

"If this Colburn comes by I'll agree to get the depositions of all four of you. How's that?"

"He may swear out a warrant for me over the spill."

"Them depositions should be enough."

"Well, he's acted kinda high-handed toward me."

"Plenty like him, they get a badge and get awfully bossy. I'll handle it if he shows up."

"Thanks," Hamp said. He gave the lawman a nod, rose and headed for his horse. He felt better about the matter with Tanner in charge. No sense in bothering a lawyer. He had other things to do.

Thunder rolled overhead and it had grown

darker since he went inside. It might even rain, he decided, stepping in the stirrup and heading for home. By the time he dropped off Hawkin's Ridge, he smiled. Shaking loose his sticky slicker to put it on, he shed the falling moisture. Been a while since he'd used it. Cold raindrops soaked through his sleeves as he dressed in it.

He wanted to go by the homeplace and check on Junie next.

Chapter 4

The first rain shower quit and moved north before he reached his homeplace. But more was on his heels as he loped Jake along the trail. He saw his wife stand up from her green garden, and a smile of warm recognition came from under the straw hat. Then with a schoolgirl look on her face, she headed for the trellis-covered gate on the run.

"You're home!" she shouted and crossed the open ground in nothing flat.

He dismounted and swept her up in his arms. She pushed back the stray hair from her face and kissed him.

"Wasn't 'specting you for a few more days. Are they good cattle you bought?"

"Thin, but they'll fatten. They ain't had much to eat. We better get to the house. That rain's following me," he said as the drops began to fall.

She shook her head to dismiss his concern. "I could stay out in it and hug you forever, Hamp Moser."

"Be better in the dry," he said as thunder went rumbling across the hill country.

"Have any trouble?" she asked.

"Some, but I got it settled."

"What was that?" She swept the hair back from her face again and looked concerned.

So he explained the shooting and the aftermath.

"Clint's going to be the death of you yet." She dropped her eyes and shook her head, with her arm in the crook of his.

"We've been together several years."

She tossed her head to get enough hair out of her eyes to see him through the raindrops. "I guess I better be grateful. Weren't for him I'd never've got you."

They made the porch and turned back to look as the shower swept over the drought-fired cornfields. He bent over and kissed her.

"I better go put up Jake." He gave the cow horse a wry look.

"Only if you promise to hurry back and"—she rolled her lips and then grinned big—"and come find me in the bed."

"I won't be long." He looked into her blue eyes and felt the magnetism.

"Good," she said, as if relieved by his answer. He tore off, with the slicker slapping his churning legs as he ran to put up the horse.

An hour later he was wearing a fresh pair of canvas pants and shirt, sipping her coffee. She was hustling around the room, fixing him food. A bandanna tied around her forehead kept her hair in place while she worked to fix his meal. The blue dress she wore fit her long hips and hugged the small breasts. Somehow the plain girl from the backwoods of Arkansas had taken on an aura of beauty. Besides, she grew great gardens, had bountiful food all the time, and made him a real wife. He'd never imagined anything like her happening in his life was even possible. He did owe Clint's wild streak for her.

"When you go to Fort Smith this fall, could I go along?" She poured fresh coffee in his cup.

He raised his chin and nodded. "Who will take care of things here?"

"Oh, I can hire someone."

"Who?" He looked through the escaping vapors at her.

"Miguel has a sister. She said she would come and care for the place, my cow and chickens. The garden would be over by then."

"No reason I'd know to hold you back, then. I'll tell Clint. I'm sure he won't mind."

She kissed him on the cheek and took the coffeepot back to the woodstove.

Tanner came by the next morning. Hamp was ready to set out for the Hayes place when the lawman showed up. The entire country had been drenched by the storm and sunup shone through the thousands of diamond-like drops on everything.

"You're out early," he said to the lawman.

"That Colburn has a sore leg."

"I told you that."

"He wants you arrested as an accomplice."

"To what?"

"Murder."

Hamp looked hard at the man. "You serving that warrant?"

"I'm trying to talk him out of it."

"Good. What about Clint?"

"He wants him for murder."

"What about those depositions?"

Elliot shook his head, took off his hat and combed his fingers through his hair. "He wants to arrest you all."

"Can he do it?"

"If he gets the judge to agree."

"That's Wilburn Needham?"

"Right."

"What'll he do?"

"I tried to talk to Needham before I left town. I hope I can get it squashed."

"It's serious then or you'd not have ridden out here to tell me this."

Elliot nodded. His face looked grim. "In case I can't get this thing stopped, you two lay low until I can get something done."

"I appreciate that."

"Guess we've known each other the biggest part of our life. You boys helped me get elected and have supported me. I owe you." The lawman reined his horse around and gave a wave before he left.

"Bad news, ain't it?" Junie said, wiping her hands on her apron and frowning at him.

"Ah, just the breaks."

"We should have offered him some food," she said as horse and rider disappeared under the hill. "That was the least I could have done for him."

Hamp hugged her shoulder. "I forgot too. I'm certain he understands."

"I hope so. I try to be friendly to folks. Don't I?"

"You're a wonderful hostess and a grand

wife, Junie." He could tell she beamed at his praise as he guided her back inside.

"You still thinking about me going to Fort Smith with you'ns?"

"I guess you want to see your paw and sister?"

"I'd sure like to go if'n I wouldn't be a burden to you."

"Well, hire the caretaker and start getting ready. We'll leave in four weeks and move these cattle slow up into the Nation. We'll graze them up there and then get to Fort Smith in late October."

She hugged him tight, swept the hair back from her face and stood on her toes to kiss him. "You're a wonderful man, Hamp Moser."

"Yeah, well, I better eat this breakfast and go find Clint."

"Oh, yeah, and you tell him—well, tell him not to get you two in any more trouble."

"We don't need that," he said, taking a seat at the table and wondering about his partner and what he was doing.

After the meal, Hamp saddled a fresh horse and headed for the Hayes place. He reached the homestead and spotted Pappy Hayes coming from the barn to the house with a pail of milk.

The older man was stooped and a toothless grin hid behind his gray stubble.

"Well, see you made 'er back."

"Yeah, Pappy, we did. Seen any of my outfit this morning?"

"Smelled Sam's cooking fire before I went to the barn to milk. They's got a camp by the biggest spring."

"You get enough fodder put up for your cow?"

"Yeah, and the team. I sure appreciated you two buying that burned up mess."

"Yesterday's rain may be the start of better times for all of us."

"Land sake's, I hope so. Looks to me like them old Messikin steers don't mind that corn being fired up."

"No, they'll eat it like it's good, no more'n they've had to eat in their lives."

"Lose any?"

"Not over five or six."

"You're lucky. Wife's got coffee on." He tossed his head toward the rock house.

"Thanks, but I better shag down to camp and see Clint."

"Good to see ya, Hamp."

He thanked Pappy, then rode the big red roan gelding he called Strawberry along the edge of the field on the creek bank. Several steers were lying down chewing their cuds near various water holes in the dry streambed. Others were still hogging down the rustling leaves and some even consumed the three-foot stalks whole. The cattle he observed did look bulging full.

At his approach, Sam straightened up from his cooking fire and wiped his hands on the apron around his waist. He handled the chuck wagon and many other matters well. Doctor, nurse, letter writer, philosopher and general good ol' boy, he knew how to feed cowboys and keep them going. Never married, he'd been a sergeant in the war, and now the old veteran liked his setup. Hamp always felt certain that with him in charge they'd be fine.

"Clint here?" Hamp asked, stepping down from his horse and hitching him to the off side of the chuck wagon.

"Sleeping." Sam handed him a cup of coffee and indicated a hump in some sogans under a cedar tree.

"We need to feed these steers some cake," Hamp said. "They'll do better and get fat faster."

"How far we got to go to get some?" Sam asked.

"Maybe San Anton. I ain't sure. Figure we can get it hauled down here, don't you?"

"Yeah, always some freighters around."

"They'd eat about a pound of cottonseed cake, every other day, it'll take seven hundred pounds to feed them."

"That's over a ton a week." Sam shook his head and spat tobacco to the side. "Won't leave much profit. Buying fired cornfields of fodder and then cake."

"It'll work. Been done before by better men than us."

"You sending Clint after the cake?" Sam asked.

"Guess he can find his way up there." Both men chuckled about his illustrious partner. "That sheriff from down there where we had the trouble wants to arrest both of us for murder," Hamp said.

"What the hell for? That was self-defense."

"You, the boy and I may have to give depositions on that."

"We can do it."

"Tanner's trying to squash it. Have to see how he does. I'm going to wake Clint up. Hell, he don't need to sleep all day."

Sam wiped the corner of his mouth with his thumb and laughed. "No need in the world."

Squatted down, Hamp poked the snoring form and waited for a response.

"Huh?" Clint sat up and blinked at him, bleary-eyed. "Oh, it's you."

"Yeah and I ain't got good news," Hamp said, busy explaining about Colburn and his efforts to have them arrested.

Sitting up cross-legged on his blankets, Clint scowled over hearing the news as he rolled himself a cigarette. He struck a gopher match on the sole of his boot and puffed away in deep concentration.

"What do I need to do?" he finally asked.

"Hook out of here for San Antonio, buy us some cake and get back here with it."

"Take me a week round-trip."

Hamp nodded. The trip would take that long anyway.

"Get four tons. We can buy more later. That's a four-week supply."

Clint frowned. "Figure they need that much?"

"Yeah, if we want them fat come October."

"What'll we do about this sheriff?"

"I think he's bed fast for a few days. I slammed him hard. Then maybe Elliot Tanner can head him off."

Clint's tongue licked his sun-cracked lips and

he grinned. "You sure must of busted him hard."

"Saved his life."

Clint laughed aloud, totally amused. "Hell-fire, you think he appreciated that?"

"He should have."

Chapter 5

The herd wasn't going to stray much from the Hayes place. So Hamp sent the Castro brothers, Pablo and Juan, to check on his own cows and calves. He instructed the two young cowboys to pack some salt up in the canyons where there was still some dry feed left, to coax the cows to range further from the dwindling water supply. Take more than one rain to make the springs go to running. Both riders knew the remote locations they needed to salt and acted grateful to get to leave the boredom of the cornfields.

Next he sent Diego Herrera, the bronc buster of the outfit on his payroll, along with the youngest vaquero, José Peppe, to help him at the ranch headquarters. Hamp had several young horses needed breaking and Diego, the handsome one, grinned big when Hamp gave him the word of his assignment. That left Sam to repair the chuck wagon and grease the axles while they were stopped. Petey could help Miguel look after the remuda and the herd.

His workers all busy, he rode over to Mark Raines's place to check on the next fired corn-field he planned to graze. Mark's fencing appeared to be holding out any range stock. He rode around a good part of it before getting to the house and corrals.

Netty Raines came out on the porch, shading her eyes with her hand against the midday glare. "That you, Hamp?"

"Yes, ma'am. Evening. How've you been?" he asked the woman in her thirties. She was showing big.

Her eyes dropped down to the swelling under her dress. "Fair enough. How's Junie? My, she sent a mess of garden things over. She's a real gardener. You got lucky, Hamp Moser, getting her."

He nodded and dismounted. "Mark ain't here?"

"No, he's digging out a spring. I'll get you a glass of water. You look thirsty."

"Sure, I'd take one. I'm going to bring the steers over in about a week to clean up the corn." He stepped up in the shade of the porch.

A cool breeze swept his face when he wiped it dry on his sleeve.

"One of the Hayes boys said you had them at their places," she said, handing him the glass. "Figured we'd be next. Sure good you boys can use that burned-up corn. We'd had a tough year otherwise."

"Tough on everyone. Clint's gone to San Antonio for some cake. When he gets back with it I expect to turn them Messikin cattle into real eaters."

"Should do it. I never get to talk much to your wife. She happy here?"

"Too busy not to be." He chuckled between sips of water.

"She's busy. Ain't in a family way yet either?"

Hamp shook his head. "Guess that'll come someday."

"Oh, it will." Netty sighed. "She'll be lucky if it ain't in the heat of the summer. Sure drags you down."

"Where are the children?" He wondered if she thought him daft for not asking sooner.

"Oh, they walked to the Rasmussens'. Having a birthday party for their eight-year-old, Wiley, and it gave me a day of peace and quiet."

"Thanks for the water. I'll tell Junie you said to be more neighborly."

"Hamp Moser, don't tell the poor girl that. Why, what would she think? She was so shy when you brought her home. How did you ever get her to say yes?"

He shook his head to dismiss her concern. "It wasn't hard."

Netty looked off across the heat waves radiating off the rustling dry cornstalks. Her eyelids drawn, she nodded her head. "I never thought you'd marry anyone. You always were so precise around women even at the schoolhouse dances. Like Mark's uncle Dave—some men seemed to like being bachelors."

"I guess it wasn't to be."

She nodded thoughtfully. "Glad you got such a sweet one. I'll tell Mark you were by. And tell her I said thanks for all the vegetables and hi."

Hamp waved to her and headed southwest for home and Junie.

When he came up from the creek and topped the rise he recognized the sweaty horse. Elliot Tanner was back. What had happened? Not good. The sheriff had plenty of other things about his job to worry about to not be at his place twice in one day. Damn, what now?

The youthful José met him and took the reins when he dismounted.

"The sheriff's here," he said in a near whisper.

"I see he is." Hamp looked hard at the house, unsure if he wanted to go another step forward. "How did the bronc busting go today?"

"Bueno, señor." Then the youth burst into a spiel in Spanish that talked about how high the horse had bucked and how far he threw Diego.

"Diego all right?"

"Oh, sí."

"Good, I better go see about the sheriff."

"Is about the man got shot in Madre County?"

Hamp nodded and headed for the front door. Long shadows reached across the ground—still hot as a fire's breath but the temperature had started toward some relief as the sun set beyond the hills.

"There's my husband." Junie's head popped up from her food preparation and she cleaned her floury hands on a towel as she rushed over to greet him.

He gave her hug and a peck on the cheek. "Elliot, you back for business or my wife's good food?"

"Little of both. Where's Clint?"

"San Anton for some cake. Why?"

"Judge Needham promised Colburn he'd hold a hearing for cause."

"Clint won't be back for a week." He stuck the dipper down in the ayolla for some water. "What does that mean?"

"I think if the three of you—Sam Hayes, that Sims boy, and you—come to town we can get this over with."

"Good. I better wash up. Looks like she's got food enough for all of us." He shook his head at all the things she had fixed for them to eat.

"Well, my lands," said Junie, "we have four cowboys, you two men and me all to eat. I sure didn't want to run out. Ring that bell. Them vaqueros, they'll be starving. I know them." She smiled at him.

"Oh, I saw Netty Raines and she thanked you for the garden stuff you sent her. Can't believe how you did it. Most folks' gardens burned up already."

"That ain't hard. I've got water."

Elliot went out to wash up with Hamp. "Lots of women could have water too. They don't want to work that hard."

Hamp agreed. "What's the judge said?"

"We need to have a hearing for cause."

Hamp lathered his hands over the wash pan. "What does that mean?"

"Means he'll listen to both sides and decide if Colburn has any cause to arrest you two."

"Clint and me?" He looked pained at the lawman beside him.

"Yeah. Colburn said you two jumped Muldoone and gunned him down."

"Why, that's crazy—I'd've left his carcass to rot out there if I had."

Elliot shook his head. "I can't do anything more than try to settle this."

Hamp knew one thing. He'd have a lawyer there. Vic Devlin would need to be in that courtroom. They weren't railroading him and Clint over this mess. He'd have good legal representation on hand if push came to shove. Somehow this incident had turned into a mushroom— maybe a poisonous one at that—and was getting bigger. He wondered what Clint was doing right then. He hoped he was well on his way to getting the cake.

Chapter 6

Sam Hayes rode a brown saddle mule, Petey Sims, the wrangler, was on a ranch horse and Hamp rode a big bay horse, Dan. They set out before sunup to be in Cedar Vale before the court proceedings started. In the cool morning, they jogged their mounts through the live oak and cedar, churning up dust. The rain's moisture had been quickly sucked up by the heat and dryness. Maybe more would come shortly. Hamp had more on his mind than rainfall. He hoped the hearing would clear up this matter once and for all.

They reached town as the stores began to open. Merchants and help were out sweeping off the boardwalks. Hamp indicated the narrow building that housed Devlin's law office. The lawyer, busy behind a paper-cluttered desk, smiled at them. He rose and shook their hands.

He was a good-sized man—Hamp guessed him to be in his forties. Devlin never had much color, being indoors all the time, and his hair was gray at the temples. He indicated the chairs that they pulled up.

"This should be over in an hour. I understand talking to Hamp that both of you saw the gunfight."

Leaning forward, Sam nodded and Petey joined him.

"Sam, tell me what you saw."

"That big galoot came riding up on his stud horse and went to shouting at Clint. Things got worse from there."

"Worse?"

"They went for their guns."

"Who drew first?"

"Looked to me like a draw."

"You four did all you could for the man?"

Sam shrugged. "Wasn't much we could do. He was dead. I took Clint to the wagon and stitched him up. Then Hamp hauled the body off to his widder."

"Petey, is it? Well, is that what you saw?"

"Yes, sir."

"Did Hamp ever draw his gun?"

"No, sir. I figured he started to go to stop them, but never got three steps."

"Good. They'll try to twist you up. You stick to your guns, guys." Devlin turned to Hamp. "I think we're ready for the hearing."

Hamp had Petey take the mounts to the livery. No telling how long the proceedings would last. Most legal things like this were drug out forever. The three men strode toward the courthouse, tipping their hats for ladies and moving aside for them.

"Clint Barton's in San Anton?" Devlin asked.

"Yes, getting cake."

"Eating cake?" Devlin teased.

"That too, probably," Sam said, walking behind them.

The courthouse interior still felt cool when Hamp entered the front doors. They crossed the lobby and went to the double oak doors. Dust particles danced in shafts of sunlight coming in the windows. The long, sheer curtains swayed in the morning breeze.

"Guess we're early," Devlin said, putting a sheaf of papers on the desk beyond the fence.

"Not too early," said Buck George, the bailiff, coming from the side room. "Judge don't aim for this to take all day."

Devlin looked to the rear of the room and turned back. "We await the sheriff, then."

"And some big prosecutor came flying in by buggy last night."

Devlin pursed his thin lips. "Who is that?"

"Thomas Sulley. Tried to get today's hearing postponed. Said he needed more time."

"What did the judge say?"

"Said we'd have it—today or else forget it."

Devlin nodded at Hamp that it would be all right. He acknowledged the man's meaning from where he sat in the first row with his men. Time passed slow and Hamp could think of a million things he could be doing besides twiddling his thumbs on a courthouse bench.

George made several trips up and down the aisle, going out in the lobby and then back, grumbling over the whereabouts of the other side. Then he went back into the judge's chambers and he did some more cussing. Loud enough all could hear. Sam shook his head and elbowed Hamp.

"They may not even come."

Hamp doubted that. Colburn had not brought that big-time prosecutor up there for nothing to happen.

The commotion at the door caused him and the others to turn. Four men were bringing someone in on a stretcher. Hamp started. He had not seen Colburn since the horse wreck.

Obviously the lawman was the one they carried past him.

"You know he was that bad off?" Hamp stood up and whispered to Devlin.

"Hell, he was on crutches two days ago. What're they going to do with him now?" the lawyer asked with a scowl.

"Someone's bringing a cot," Sam said, indicating the bearer in the back.

They planned to make a real show of it for the judge. Hamp had not come in on a wagonload of melons. He knew what this prosecutor had in mind for the day. But why all this for a man like Muldoone?

The lawyer wore a snowy white shirt with ruffles and a silk tie with a diamond stickpin. His dark suit was tailored and his shoes looked like polished stone. He acted like he was above anything in the courtroom, especially the folks who had been filtering in to make up the audience, many of them friends that Hamp knew well.

"My dear boy," Sulley said to Colburn, looking down at the prone lawman like one looked at a dying friend, "I hope these hearings aren't too much for you today."

In a dry, cracked voice, Colburn said, "I'll do my best, Thomas."

Hamp glanced at the tin ceiling tiles for celestial help. He shook his head to cut off the about-to-bluster-out-loud Sam. This had all the makings of a day he would not soon forget.

A fly buzzed around Hamp's head as the frilly-shirted prosecutor rambled on and on about the cold-blooded, back-shooting, violent murder of the best citizen in Madre County, Roscoe Muldoone. His dusty boots stretched out, Hamp slumped on the bench. His spurs clinked lightly whenever he made a small move.

"Your Honor?" Devlin finally stood up. "The honorable Mister Sulley has been over this ground enough to plant turnips. May I please present the witnesses to this man's unfortunate demise? The men that were there and can tell the real story of what happened that day."

"Your Honor—" Sulley approached the bench. "These men have flaunted the law. That is why the chief lawman of Madre County is bedridden at this trial. He was ran over by these men while performing his duty."

"I object!" Devlin shouted. "He was overusing his authority and blatantly tried to arrest someone that had nothing to do with this incident you are so upset about."

Purple veins popped out on Judge Wilburn Needham's clean-shaven face. The red tinge shot up into his cheeks from his hard-set jawline as he pounded the gavel.

"Mr. Sulley, you have indeed made your point. Be seated. Swear in your first witness, Mr. Devlin."

"I call Hampton Moser to the stand."

The interrogation went smoothly. Devlin led the way and Hamp felt the truth was told. When Devlin turned and said to the judge, "That is all, Your Honor. That is the story of that day."

"Mr. Sulley? You wish to cross-examine?"

"I do, Your Honor." The lawyer jerked down his vest and started across the room.

"Do you drink, sir?" he asked.

"On an occasion, yes."

"Were you drinking on that day?"

"No, sir."

"I have a witness that said she could smell liquor on your breath that evening."

"Mrs. Muldoone?" Hamp frowned at the man.

"I have a witness that said you were drinking. Were you or were you not drinking on the night of Roscoe Muldoone's murder?"

"It was not murder."

"Answer my question."

"No, I was not drinking on the day of Muldoone's death."

So the day drug on, Sulley's accusations grinding a little deeper each time into Hamp's diminishing patience. The sheriff lying there on the cot holding the back of his hand to his forehead and making a small groan or two to punctuate Sulley's persistence and Devlin's growing objections. They took a lunch break and despite the judge's warning for Sulley to get through, the afternoon crawled on, with Hamp in the hard chair.

At six o'clock, Judge Needham adjourned the hearing until the next morning. Hamp left the witness chair angry and stiff from sitting so long and wondering how Sulley would try to twist his words.

"What's all this going to prove, anyway?" Sam demanded, filling his mouth with a chew as they left the courthouse. The four men carried Colburn out on his stretcher and went past them.

"For two bits I'd set his ass on fire and we'd see how torn up he really is," Sam said after they went by.

"I agree. Petey, you better get on home," Hamp said. "But be back here tomorrow."

"They going to ask me all those questions and tangle me up like they tried to do you?" the youth asked.

"Petey, tell them what you know. That's all you have to do."

"Sure, Hamp, but I'm scared of that man."

"He can't kill you or eat you."

"Naw, but I might worry he could."

Devlin joined them. "Got some good news. Judge said in there just now that the hearing will be over tomorrow. Sorry you had to stay in town."

"What do you think?" Hamp asked.

"Sulley has no evidence. It's all circumstantial. I think Needham will throw it out."

"I hope so. Thanks," Hamp said and Devlin excused himself with a wave. Hamp and Sam headed for the Laredo Saloon.

"Good thing you sent Clint off," Sam said, before he pushed inside the bat-wing doors. "He'd've blown up at that frilly-shirted bag of wind."

"That's what he wanted," Hamp said and they went inside.

They ate supper in the saloon, had a few drinks and took a room at the Blair Hotel. Hamp's mind was on Junie, the cattle herd and the plan to fatten them enough to fill the bill at Fort Smith. Stretched out on his back, he looked at the small hammock of cobwebs in the corner of the ceiling in the hot room. A breeze finally came in the open window and swept over him. He wished the trial business was over and he could get on with his life. Be much better to be trailing steers than lollygagging around there.

He drew in a deep breath, thinking about his wife and her willowy body. Damn, what a wasted night. He rolled over and went to sleep.

Before court started the next day, Sheriff Colburn sat up in a blanket-covered chair beside Sulley at his table. His right arm was now in a sling, which perplexed Hamp as well as Sam, who frowned hard at the lawman.

"They drop him off the stretcher?" Sam asked with a chuckle.

"His arm was fine yesterday. Had the back of that hand on his forehead," Hamp whispered.

"I know. You seeing the crowd we're gathering?" Sam indicated the courtroom onlookers filing in.

Hamp nodded and they all stood as the judge entered.

Court was called to order and Needham called both lawyers to the bench.

"Whatever you wish to present will be done in the next four hours. Am I clear?" the judge asked the attorneys.

"Yes, Your Honor. I wish to charge this

Hampton Moser with attempted murder of a peace officer. I want him handed over to the local sheriff and held."

"You may swear out a warrant with the sheriff. I will not order Mr Moser held. The sheriff will serve the papers. There will be another hearing. Do you have witnesses?"

"I am—"

"In Madre County you are a prosecutor. In Kerr-Mac County, you are an individual citizen, as is the sheriff. Mr. Moser has his rights, too. The fact that you have no grand jury warrants or findings in this case and are on a fishing trip in my courtroom does not escape me, Mr. Sulley."

"I object."

"Object all you want. Get this matter on the record and get through by twelve o'clock."

At noontime, Sully was still ranting and raving at Sam on the stand. The judge dropped his gavel and gave each lawyer five minutes to sum up.

When they finished, Needham sat back in the chair. "I see nothing here that indicates foul play on the part of the men you have called here, Mr. Sulley. They are hardworking, honorable men who have expressed their regret over the loss of Mr. Muldoone's life. Thus I am dismissing the hearings."

"What about my charges against Moser?" Sulley shouted.

"See the sheriff."

"This is an outrage. A miscarriage of justice!"

"Mr. Sulley, one more outburst from you and I'll hold you in contempt of court."

The crowd laughed. Needham closed it down.

Hamp rose and shook Devlin's hand.

"For a man just off his deathbed, I'm proud to see him walking—"

When Colburn reached the gate, he glared at Hamp, his dark eyes sharp as diamonds. "I'll see you dead, Moser."

"Next time I won't knock you down with a horse either," Hamp said.

He stood for a long time staring at the back of the lawman. What was the meaning in all this? Was Muldoone a close friend or what? His mind went back to the day he delivered the body to Kathren. She was a vindictive enough person— those two acted the same.

Chapter 7

"Don't tell me I missed all the fun," Clint teased. The wagonloads of whole cottonseed had begun to arrive. No cake was available, according to Clint, and the next best thing was the fuzzy, unprocessed seed. Hamp was anxious to get the Mexican cattle started eating it. They transferred four burlap sacks from the freighters to the farm wagon and took it into the mowed-down stalks.

Sam drove, with Hamp and Clint in the back. They tailgated a bag, leaving a gray band of the seed on the ground. Soon a few curious animals came over, sniffing the strong aroma. It was like a signal—we ain't being left out, others seemed to say, and joined them. Soon the steers were chewing mouthfuls of the seed.

Hamp nodded at his partner in approval, then spoke to the driver. "Go ahead, Sam. We'll put out the rest."

They dumped the remainder out in a long

swath. By this time the steers were flocking in to eat it. So the feeding began. Hamp was looking for Elliot to ride out any day and serve a warrant, perhaps on both of them. The longer Elliot took to get there, the less chance he had of catching him in Texas. They'd get on the move north to the grass in a few weeks.

If this cattle-feeding business worked like he thought it would, the cottonseed would cost only twenty dollars a ton and five dollars freight—a bargain. They should stand to make a respectable profit on this drive. He planned to buy more land with his share.

By late afternoon he had parted with his partner for the day and was headed for the homeplace, the big bay he called Topper set in a trot. The wagon tracks were dry and Topper churned up some acrid dust with his hooves. Some crows scolded Hamp and he grinned at the noisy ones.

In the long rays of sundown piercing the cedars on the hills with an orange fire, he could make out a rider's silhouette. He drew up Topper and wondered who waited in the road.

"Hamp?" He recognized the man as Tate McDaniels, a cowboy in his thirties.

Hamp nodded. "How you been, Tate?"

"I wanted you to know word's out they've put money out for you and Clint dead."

"Who?"

"I ain't sure. Word's out and I heard it over at Shade's. You know there's been a couple of misunderstandings about me. But I rode over here hoping to catch you. You always done me right, Hamp. I'd've hated to have known there was dry gulchers after you and you not known about it."

"Figure they'd shoot me in the back?"

"That's the kind a folks they'd be."

"Come up to the house. Junie will feed us."

Tate shook his head and looked around like a man on the run. "Thanks, but I better be moving on."

"Wait," Hamp said and dug in his pocket. He came up with some money, then he rode in close to the man and shoved it in his vest pocket, knowing he'd never take it any other way. "Thanks, pard. Ride easy."

A little money for a friend on the dodge was all. He owed Tate that much. Now he searched over the country covered in the bloody gasp of sundown. Shades of red and copper painted the back of the rider as he went off on a side track and soon disappeared in the cedars.

He would need to be more careful of where and how he went places after this. They'd wait for him at the usual ones. Junie, I'll be there shortly.

Chapter 8

Hamp milked Junie's cow for her. In the cool of early morning, he listened to the Jersey's rough tongue lick the bottom of the holey dishpan for any more feed. Seated on the one-legged stool, and with the strong aroma of the bovine penetrating his nose, he squirted streams of snowy milk into the pail under the occasional flip of her hard tail. Bobwhite quail called to him from off in the brambles and moved about in the stickery security, no doubt anxious to rush over and peck at the minute leavings of Bossy's cereal breakfast.

Bossy raised her head and let out a long, lonesome bawl for her companions. One answered, her yearling half-Durham heifer down by the creek. This year's progeny poked his head through the pen fence and strained in jealousy for milk himself, his plaintive cries short and juvenile.

The chore completed, Hamp stripped out the last dribble and patted her on the hip as he stood. "You can go now."

The whine of the shot cut close like a mad stinging bee. Hamp tossed the pail of milk and scrambled for the cover of the shed. Bossy left at a half run and he realized, crawling for a place behind the corral, that he carried no sidearm on his hip. Two more shots slapped into the calf shed and one whined over the corral above him. Only thing he had going for him was the shooters were not great shots. Grateful for their ineptness, he laid tight on the ground.

"Hamp! Hamp!"

"Stay there, for God's sake, Junie. I'm fine!"

"Where are they?" she shouted to him from the house.

"Above the garden somewhere."

"You sure you're all right?"

"I'm fine. You stay down."

He could hear her rummaging and tearing up things inside the house. He couldn't see the shooters, didn't know it they'd moved or not. But he suspected they were on a high point above the garden in some thick cedars. They'd brought the war to him—something he'd never have worried about before he got her.

Two great blasts came from the side window

of the house. A horse on the hillside screamed in pain and men began cursing. Hamp scrambled to his feet and broke for the front door on a dead run, keeping low and hoping the confusion of her shooting the shotgun would cover his movements. The last ten steps, someone cut down on him. Bullets sprayed dust on him. But he dove in the open door and her shotgun cut loose again as he raised up from the floor.

Junie stood backed away from the window with the scattergun broken open as she ejected the spent casings.

"Them sons a bitches," she muttered under her breath and jammed two more brass twelve-gauge shells in the chamber and snapped it shut. "You all right?"

"I'm fine. You get down so they can't shoot you."

"I'll get down when I blow them to kingdom come. Who are they anyway?" She started back for the window.

"Hired killers."

"I'll hired kill them." She took aim with her right elbow stuck out to the side, then squeezed off a shot that roared in the house.

Someone yelled in protest. She emptied the second barrel in the same direction and they went to screaming. She broke the shotgun open again, shook her head. By then Hamp was beside her, hugging her shoulder and dragging her out of harm's way. "Easy, easy. I think from the sounds of things you've got one or more of them hard."

"Come around here—shooting at my man— I'll hound them devils to hell."

"I'm going to scout around them. You stay down here, don't get shot, and I'll circle them."

She nodded in approval. "You need this scattergun?"

"Nope." He strapped on the holster and checked the loads in his Colt. "I'll use this."

She turned her ear to listen. "They're getting away."

"Good," he said and holstered the handgun. Suited him fine if they never came back.

"You reckon we got some of them?" Her blue eyes looked deep into his.

"I reckon we did. A couple of them sure sounded hit." He hugged and kissed her. "Damn, girl, they get you mad your Arkansas blood comes to the top. Sorry, but I lost that bucket of milk."

"I'm just proud they missed you. I'll feed the calf something. He'll be all right and you're all right. That's all that matters." She pressed her face against his shirt. "Land sakes, why're they wanting to kill you? This a feud?"

"Must be."

"Well, I know about them kinda deals. They got lots of them up home in Arkansas. Folks killing each other over nothing is what I don't know about."

"Neither do I."

"Be careful," she said after him as he went to scout the hillside to learn what he could about them.

He searched on the ground atop the rise. From their tracks in the dirt, he could tell the shooters wore boots. They'd obviously been there a while. Several roll-your-own butts littered the ground and showed where they had waited behind the cedar tree screen. One had run-down heels and a hole in his boot sole.

Squatted on his heels, Hamp studied the cracked horseshoe print from one of their mounts. It was a small-footed pony. Someone, like a blacksmith, might recall that animal and put a name or face to it.

This all had to do with the Muldoone shooting. Why was someone so set upon revenge? Did that woman Kathren hire them?

He stood and looked across the country. Sure needed some more rain. Maybe it would come.

One shower was never enough. He drew a deep breath and headed for the house. They'd need to move the steers to the next corn patch in the morning. Those hungry critters were mowing it down faster than he'd calculated. At this rate, they'd be heading for the Nation in a few weeks. He could sure hope that there was grass up there to finish putting the weight on them.

"Learn anything?" she asked, meeting him at the doorway.

"One wears worn-out boots and they have a cracked shoe on a hind foot of one of their horses."

Junie laughed and then curled her lower lip under her front teeth. "Ain't exactly a pitcher of 'em, is it?"

"No, but it's a lead. They also roll their own and smoke a lot."

"They were up there all night?" Her blue eyes opened wide in shock.

He nodded, then reached out and hugged her. "They won't be trouble to us long."

"They get in range of my shotgun, they better have their business with their maker all made up."

"Maybe they ought to talk to the coyotes." Hamp chuckled at the memory of the chicken stealers' demise.

"Yeah, but they ain't around no more to warn them." She gave a hard glare at the cedar-covered hill and they went inside.

Late afternoon, Hamp swung by town after checking on the cattle. He'd told Sam and Miguel they'd move the herd the next day. His partner, Clint, was off making arrangements to unload the new cottonseed that had arrived. Hamp hoped to go over the matter of the shooters with Clint and see Elliot about what the law would do about them.

In Cedar Vale, Hamp saw the blacksmith first. He dismounted at the front of the shed and the array of buildings that Bart McNab used for his business.

Powerfully built, McNab had arms swollen with muscles. He was hammering away on a piece of steel on his anvil but paused and nodded to Hamp.

"Afternoon. You got your legal business straight?" the big man asked, looking grateful for someone to talk to.

"So far. Judge dismissed their charges."

"Plenty of folks like me were ready to kick that jailhouse door in if'n they'd tried to keep you two."

"Glad we didn't need you. Anyone been by

with a horse needing a hind shoe replaced that's split?"

Bart sliced the sweat from his face with a finger. "A small dish-faced sorrel?"

"I ain't sure of the color."

"Three gent left her here about an hour ago. Going to swing by and get her tonight."

"You know them?"

"Never laid eyes on them, but one of them accidentally got hisself shot while they were hunting."

"My wife plastered them with buckshot."

"What the hell they shooting at her for?"

"They were shooting at me."

"What for?"

"Kinda of what I'd like to know. Seen Clint?"

"He's over at the Alamo. Rode in an hour ago."

Hamp nodded, looking down the street at the horses standing hip-shot at the rack. "I better alert him. If they can't arrest us they're trying to kill us."

"Figure it was the law from down there?"

"I doubt it was the law, but I don't know of anyone else that is that mad at us."

"How's them steers doing?"

"Doing fine. Eating that seed and stalks they're really filling up."

"Damn neat idea." Bart shook his head. "If it would ever rain."

With a grim set to his mouth, Hamp agreed. "See you."

"About those guys and this sorrel horse?" Bart gave a head toss toward the waiting animal.

"I was going to talk to Clint about them and come back. What did they look like?"

"Cowboys. One was twenty or so. The other maybe thirty. A tall, thin guy. He sucked on a straw all the time he was here."

"I thought there might have been three?"

"Yeah, the shot one was all bent over sitting in the saddle. Guess they took him to Doc Hicks."

"I'll be checking. Thanks."

"I'll be sure and not ever upset your Arkansas wife," Bart teased as Hamp went out in the sunshine and unhitched his horse.

"She might shoot you," he said with a grin and mounted up.

Hamp found his partner in the Alamo Saloon, seated at a table with two other ranchers, Albert Cravens, an older man, and Krinkie Salsbury, who was in his thirties.

"Bring any rain with you?" Cravens asked, leaning back in his chair.

With a smile, Hamp shook his head and took a chair. "Not where I've been."

"Everything all right at the cow camp?" Clint asked over his schooner of beer.

"Fine. We better move them tomorrow. They've mowed down most of that field."

"I hired the Montoya boy to haul out the seed. He's got a wagon and team. I'll tell him we're moving to Randy's, huh?"

"Good as any. Say, three birds came by and took shots at me this morning."

The other two leaned forward to listen and Clint frowned. "What the hell for?"

"Guess they were hired to do that. Not a very neat job. Junie shot one of them. Bart thinks they took him to Dr. Hicks."

"Guess we better go hunt them down."

Hamp held up his hands to stop his partner. "I want Elliot to handle it."

"You tell him about it?"

"I'm working that way. Wanted to talk to you first."

"Let's go find him. What did they look like?"

After he described them, the two ranchers excused themselves and Hamp thanked the men for their offer of help if they needed any. They promised to be in touch.

"Elliot will be home eating supper at this time of day," Clint said as they left.

"Yeah." Hamp wished he was home with Junie doing the same thing. He unhitched the reins and swung up a little stiffer than before.

The sheriff's house was a small frame one with a yard fence. They dismounted and started up the walk. Elliot came out sucking on a toothpick.

"Seen you two coming, I figured I better get out here. What's wrong?"

Chapter 9

Hamp's eyes felt gritty as a sandpile. His mind was stuffed with cobwebs and his feet struck the floor punctuated by a huge yawn. Damn, the sun wasn't even up.

"I've got your breakfast ready." Junie stood in the doorway, outlined by the lamplight coming from the kitchen.

"Coming," he said, shaking out a sock. All he knew about the would-be shooters was the one packing Junie's buckshot was named Crews. Doc thought he'd live. Crews didn't have much else to say, and his two pards had already drifted away. They never came back for the sorrel mare at Bart's. After dumping Crews at the doc's they lit a shuck for parts unknown. Elliot had promised to look for them and keep interrogating the wounded one. Hamp had told Junie all about it when he got back home after midnight.

"You all moving those steers today?" she asked.

"That's why I'm up," he said, holding his hand over his yawn. Standing, he finished dressing and smiled at her when she advanced toward him.

She used her index finger to poke him in the chest. "You watch out. Them devils will try it again. They ain't through with trying to shoot you. I know their kind."

"They'll be pushing up bluebells if they try."

"Bluebells or no bluebells, you be careful." Then she hugged him. "Oh, I could keep you here. But them cattle would never get moved and the world won't stand still for it."

"I promise I'll be back early today."

She looked up at him. "You just come back, Hamp Moser."

"Yes, ma'am."

The horse he selected was a cold-backed dun and he bucked hard enough that the four hands riding with him laughed at his antics. Once he lined the dun out, they rode at a hard trot in the gray predawn for the Raines place.

Clint and the others were around the campfire finishing breakfast. Sam held up the granite pot, offering them some coffee and the whole crew nodded as they dismounted.

Hamp still had the yawns and noticed his partner, Clint, was little better.

"Going to be a long day for such a simple job," Clint complained, getting up stiff like, heading for the pen and the horses that Petey had cut out for them.

"A real long one."

The cattle drove easy enough, tamed down over their time in the cornfield, and by midafternoon the herd was settled in a fresh field of drought-fired cornstalks. The boy Clint had hired was bringing seed for them in the morning. They'd get tamer than a house dog at this rate, Hamp decided, watching them devour the sheaths and then the stalks.

"Why don't you take a day or so and catch up at home?" Clint asked. "Sam, Miguel and I can handle these cattle. Get all you want done. Two weeks we're going to have to head north. I can't believe what this bunch can consume in a day. Especially since we went to feeding them that cake."

"That seed's making them hungry enough to eat fence rails," Hamp said with a smile. "I'll fix up Junie a wagon and camp outfit."

"Yeah, we can handle this."

Hamp started for home. The Mexican boys wanted to go by town and get some things, so he rode alone. Be nice to have some time to catch up, though he doubted he would ever really reach that point. He always had more than enough to fix up if he ever could find any time.

Junie ran from the house, looking pleased at his homecoming, and walked with him to the corral to unsaddle the dun.

"Everything fine here today?" he asked.

She nodded.

"You all right?" he asked, lifting the saddle off the sweaty dun.

She made a whimsical face at him. "I was thinking maybe I'd have some news for you."

"What was that?" He slipped off the bridle and turned the dun loose.

She squinted her eyes and looked at him. "I thought I was going to have a baby. But—I ain't."

"Well, damn, girl, guess we'll have to work harder at it." He swept her up in his arms and headed for the house. "Like right now!"

"Why, land sakes—where are them boys?" She cranked her head around to look for them.

"Town. Ain't no one here but us chickens."

She put her arms around his neck and nodded smugly. "We better do that."

*   *   *

The time passed swiftly. No rain—though distant storms lighted the night sky, no drops fell on them. He found a team of matched blacks for her rig, a smaller wagon than Sam's. Bart McNab had some ash bows for it and a new canvas top. So she was soon well fixed for the trip. Her Mexican family moved in one of the empty *jacals* and learned all about her milk cow and chickens.

Hamp kept an eye open, but he saw no sign of the other two bushwhackers. Elliot came by to say the wounded one pleaded guilty to a charge of aggravated assault and got three years. But Crews never said the names of the other two—claimed he had only met them on the road. Said they just helped him to the doctor's office.

Elliot shook his head and apologized. "Best I could do."

"Thanks. Least he ain't out here shooting at me."

The two men parted and Hamp went back to the house.

"I'm plumb excited about going on this trip," Junie said when he walked in the room.

"I expect you'll get plumb bored as slow as we're going."

She pursed her lips and shook her head. "No way, not with you."

The aroma of her cooking made his mouth water. He shook his head in disbelief—it'd been a lucky deal for him getting her. He studied her backside as she worked at the stove. Sure not bad to look at her willowy body. A man could do much worse than Junie.

Time flew by and Hamp knew they better get headed north; with the dried-up corn patches about consumed, they needed to move on. So with Junie's people in place they set out for the herd the next morning. The boys herded the re-placement horses along, Hamp drove the black team and she sat up on the seat with him.

The first afternoon Clint's man showed up with enough cottonseed for three feedings and they shoved out a third of it to the steers. The longhorns licked the ground where they left the long ribbon of dull white seed. They planned to have seed for them all the way past San Anton.

Closer to Austin, the returning drovers said, there was grass available. Clint rode ahead to check on things. The sooner they could cut out feeding the seed the sooner they'd save the ex-pense of it. Meanwhile the steers were licking their sides and turning up shiny hair, so Hamp felt good that they were gaining and doing so well.

A week later, north of the Colorado River, they struck some good grazing and they spent a day letting the steers fill and then half a day driving them. This meant they only made ten to twelve miles, but the cattle were putting on lots of flesh fast.

Whenever they paused to let them graze a day, Junie chased down wild plums in the thickets, made jelly and plum pastries for the delighted crew. Soon on the days when the herd laid over they helped her pick fruit. Hamp thought she blossomed out as the head of the fruit brigade. A smile on her lips and the stains of the purple treasure on her faded dress, she made large batches in her kettles.

Their steers were a small herd by the standards of the big outfits going north to Kansas and the railhead all summer long with herds in the thousands. When they reached Fort Worth, Hamp took her to town and she bought material for a new dress to wear when she got home. He found her a new straw hat, though her face was a rich brown from going without one all the time.

Sleeping under the wagon at night and enjoying themselves, they rode off double from time to time and took privates baths in some pothole. Idyllic days were passed on the Trinity River until it was time to head north for the Red River crossing and the Nation. They sent both wagons over by ferry and the snag-dotted river was low enough that except for the quicksand, the crossing was uneventful.

A few head needed to be snaked out, but all made it over, though the mired ones wore some mucky brown coating. Headed east by northeast, they used the headed-out bluestems that stood taller than a man for the cattle to feed on. East of the main trail, Clint had found better forage and the steers soon became harder to drive, a sign that Hamp knew meant they were getting in fat under those multicolored hides.

Squatted down on his boot heels, Clint smoked a roll-your-own and nodded in approval. "We'll head for Boggy Station in the morning."

"You following the old Butterfield Stage tracks?" Hamp asked.

"Yeah. Course, it might rain."

"Been more rain up here than at home anyway."

"Sure is a damn sight greener here than at home."

Thick clouds shut off the sun at dawn. When

the chuck wagon and Junie's wagon were hitched they started northeast. Hamp recognized most of the landmarks as the bellowing herd began the day's trek. Thunder grumbled off in the south and he hoped that Junie and her team kept up with Sam and the mules. The herd moving, he waved to the swing riders to head them out. The others began filing as his hands sat horseback waiting for them to take shape so they could do their respective jobs. The ribbon soon was moving in a good formation. Another day in the life of drovers headed for Fort Smith.

Rain, thunder and lightning battered them by midmorning, the sheets of rain diminishing Hamp's vision. More tail-enders forced Hamp to join Peppe at the rear and whip the laggards. Their hides slick with water and the wind driving in their faces, the steers looked for any excuse to stop and the two riders had to fight them hard.

The cold penetrated Hamp's oilskin slicker, drawing goose bumps on his skin under his shirt. He shivered as he spurred the horse into the stupid slowpokes. Miguel joined them, shouting at one on the other side. The job appeared hopeless. One moved and another stopped and forced Hamp to saw the bay around and go back for that one.

"Hamp! Hamp!"

He turned in the hard downpour and blinked at Clint shouting at him. "It's Junie. She's gone!"

"Where's the wagon?" A knife stabbed his heart. His partner had to be wrong. She was only away from her rig.

"It's a mile ahead—abandoned. No sign of her." The flush of the wind tore his words away.

"You certain?" He tried to see Clint's face in the unrelenting rain. If anything had happened to her—there'd be hell to pay. *Gawd, don't let her be hurt!*

Chapter 10

Hamp squatted on his spurs. Smoke from the fire ring stung his eyes. Across from him, the old Indian had deep lines eroded in his saddle-leather face. Only his sharp black eyes held any life as they peered out of the hunched-up hull of a once proud warrior huddled on the ground under a trade blanket for warmth.

"Someone took my woman two days ago," Hamp said.

"Bad business to take someone's woman."

"Three men. Lost their trail."

"White men or Indians?"

"I ain't seen them. All I seen was some tracks—two of them wore boots."

Hamp shifted his weight to his other foot. Had this old man seen them pass? They could have ridden right by his shelter of canvas strung by ropes from some sycamore trees and poles.

Still, he figured those diamond eyes didn't miss much, and waited for a reply.

The old man nodded. "Two white men and one breed."

"That could be them. They have a woman with them?"

He bobbed his head. "Had her wrapped in blanket, but her hands were tied—I could see that."

Thank God, she was still alive. What next? The tracks he had followed for a day were theirs. Someone was looking out for him.

"They ride south?"

"Cross river here." He motioned with a gnarled hand toward the brown stream.

"How long ago?"

"Last night at dark."

Hamp wet his cracked lips. Good. They weren't an insurmountable distance ahead of him.

"You eat food," the old man said and a fat older woman with a blanket for a skirt and her flat breasts exposed delivered him some steaming meat on a bark tray.

The Indian waving at him to do as he said, Hamp surrendered and sat on the ground. Mumbling thanks to her, he accepted the food. He had not eaten in so long, he had forgotten the last time. While he needed it, he knew if he ate much his burning stomach would reject it.

"Good," he said after he picked up the first piece and put it in his mouth. "Was one a tall man?"

"Tall man." The old man nodded.

"My name's Hamp Moser."

"Me Ramey Horsekiller. Glad to meet you, Hamp."

"Same here. Can I hire an Indian tracker around here?"

Horsekiller nodded. "I go with you."

Hamp considered him for a long moment. "You feel up to long hours riding?"

"Me plenty tough old Cherokee."

What choice did he have? Junie was out there in the hands of those dumb bushwhackers—at least he considered them the prime suspects of her abduction. Hell only knew what they had already done to her. "You be ready to ride in a little while."

"Sleep. Go early. Rest your horse now. Squaws rub him down. Feed him grain. We make more steps when we are rested."

"I don't need to rest. I need to find her."

"We will find them quicker if they think you have lost their trail."

Hamp shook his head. What did he mean?

"They want you to follow or else they would have lost you."

"So you think they want to ambush me?" He looked hard out of his right eye at Horsekiller, the smoke from the fire about to make it tear.

The Indian shrugged and then he nodded.

"Guess you're right. How do we prevent that?"

The old man smiled. "Maybe let them sleep too."

Throw them off their guard must be what he meant. Hamp wasn't sure of anything. The old woman's food had set well in his gut anyway, despite his concern over it. If only they could find his Junie and get her away from those men. It had been eating him up ever since he found her empty wagon.

At sunup, he discovered his horse was resaddled and so was a motheaten-looking gray, standing beside a long yearling bay colt with a pack on it. The old woman under a blanket carried buckets of water back from the river. She passed him without a word and entered the shelter. He wondered if Horsekiller was ready to go.

The old man came out wearing a beat-up cowboy hat with a eagle feather and handed him a turtle-shell bowl. "Eat food. Maybe damn long time before we eat again."

Hamp used the small wooden dipper and tasted the sweetened cornmeal mush. He nodded in approval to the man and began feeding himself.

The woman took the bowls and went back inside. Looking ready to go, Horsekiller carried an old trapdoor rifle and used a black blanket for a coat. They mounted and crossed the river. It was barely belly deep, but the colt had to swim in a place or two. Unconcerned, Horsekiller dragged the young horse along and they climbed the bank. He bent over in the saddle and read the tracks. Satisfied, he nodded and they went south across the rolling grassland.

"Where can they go this way?"

"Whiskey."

"Whiskey who?"

"Go buy whiskey."

"Reckon that's where they're going?" He must mean some bootlegger who lived off in this direction. In an hour, they crossed a set of well-used wagon tracks that ran east and west. Horsekiller studied them, then as if satisfied, he set out for some post oak timber on a ridge.

"They headed for this whiskey?" he asked when the old man stopped on the crest.

"They might be there now." He dropped off his horse. "We wait for night to go see them."

Hamp couldn't decide if that was a plan or if the old man was simply worn out from riding hard all day. Rather than argue, he decided to let things develop. First they had crossed ground all day that he could never have tracked even an elephant over. If the old man was that good he sure needed him. He felt he better cut Horsekiller some slack and wait to see how it went.

They ate some peppered jerky. It was fiery hot, but it beat the nothing in his own saddlebags. They ever got near a store or town, he'd buy them some food; until then whatever his tracker had was going to have to do them.

He dozed a little with his back to the rough bark of a post oak. Horsekiller slept on a blanket on the ground like he was at home. Hamp hoped he didn't do so all night. The moon rose. Some owls went to hooting and a red wolf howled. Horsekiller sat up.

"Time to go now."

Whatever clock he used, Horsekiller acted rested and ready in the darkness to ride forever. That suited Hamp. He wanted this business over as quick as possible. Clint and the boys could deliver those cattle to Fort Smith, he had no doubt. It was Junie he wanted back.

The cow pony Hamp had selected was a tough, tall bay. Lots of bottom and always dropped his head and ate when the chance came. He'd learned long ago a worrying horse that fretted all the time when a man stopped and didn't eat at the opportunity would soon tire on the trail. The boys called him Chance and that meant there was a chance he'd buck. The hard ride had taken that out of him, but he still had plenty of bottom when Hamp swung in the saddle.

"How far?"

"Not long ways. These guys are plenty tough."

"Ones got my wife or the ones make whiskey?"

"Whiskey ones tough. I don't know them others."

Hamp nodded, satisfied, and looked across the wide-open sea of grass. The land grew hillier. The hollers between these sweeping tops were dark with timber. A deer fled from them and an owl plucked a screaming rabbit in its talons and soundlessly its wings carried it away.

Horsekiller paused on a ridge and pointed to the dark outline of an outfit beneath them. A few buildings and pens in the moonlight were obvious. They took their horses back out of sight and hobbled them.

Hamp checked his Colt and made certain it was loaded. He took some extra .44 cartridges from his saddlebag to put in his vest pocket and a smaller loaded .30-caliber Colt he stuck in his belt. Armed, he nodded to the Indian.

"Tough sumbitches." Horsekiller repeated his warning.

"I like them that way. But I don't want her hurt if they do try to shoot it out."

Horsekiller nodded that he understood and they started off down the hill. Hamp would have gone down in the bottom and come from that way rather than risk crossing the open grassy slope. But unless someone looked up their way, this might be the best approach and the least-expected way. The tall dry grass had a rich odor that went up his nose. Some spring-footed grasshoppers popped off as if awakened by them. If there were any lights on in the buildings they were dim.

He felt better when they could smell pig shit. They stopped behind a building and listened to several pigs snoring in their sleep. Hamp dried the palm of his gun hand on his canvas pants. Horsekiller eased along and around the rail fencing. He bent over and peered in the pen. Several hip shot horses stood in the corral.

"They left the crippled one here." He pointed out a horse holding up a front foot.

Did that mean the kidnappers were gone? Hamp looked around as the old man carefully moved along the corral. Seeing nothing, he stood back when Horsekiller set down his rifle and began sliding out the bars that served as a gate.

"No horses, no follow."

"Good idea," Hamp said in a whisper, picking up the rifle, ready to hand it back when Horsekiller finished. Waving his arm, the old man herded the horses quietly out the gate and they left in a slow trot. He took the Springfield back and gave a head toss toward the house.

"I owe these bastards."

Hamp accepted his words with a nod and followed. The front door was open on what he decided must be the living quarters. There was some candlelight inside, but not much. They walked slow toward the porch. Out of nowhere a low-snarling dog charged the old man with bite on his mind. He took a swift rifle butt to the head with a clunk and a short whine. The furry dog lay still. Horsekiller never looked back at it.

Rifle ready, he centered his attention on that door and anything else that moved at the house.

They were in the open for thirty feet to the dark porch. Hamp set each step down softly, and though he couldn't match the old warrior's stealth, he came close. At the porch they stopped. Horsekiller held up three fingers and then took hold of his rifle. He stepped on the stoop and the board creaked ever so much. Then he took another and Hamp, with a check at their back side to be certain they were alone, joined him.

Horsekiller indicated he wanted him at the window. With care, Hamp moved over there. From his position, he could see someone sitting at the table.

"A good night to die," Horsekiller said and his rifle roared. The blast threw the man at the table over backward and snuffed out the light.

With his Colt cocked in his fist Hamp felt his heart thump like a sledgehammer as he viewed the pitch-dark room. Then he heard someone swear in the side room and burst out, blasting away. Two shots from Hamp's .44 stopped him.

Then a woman screamed. His heart stopped for a moment. It wasn't Junie's voice.

Horsekiller lighted some candles on the table and the ashen face of a breed woman in a night

shift appeared in the side doorway. The second
bootlegger was sprawled facedown and she
tripped over his body, but not before Hamp
kicked his handgun across the dirt-floored room
so she couldn't retrieve it. Shaken from her fall,
she raised up on her knees, looked with fear
from one to the other. She appeared to be in her
twenties, short, with eyes that slanted at the corners, two deep scars on her cheeks and thick
lips.

"Who are you?" she asked in a shaky voice.

"My sons' name was Horsekiller," he said to
her.

She looked paler and wrung her hands on the
oversize garment's material. "I had nothing to
do with that."

"Three men were here earlier. And a
woman?" Horsekiller demanded.

Still on her knees, she nodded woodenly.

"Was she all right?" Hamp asked her.

She looked at him, blinking her dark eyes as
if in a trance, finally said, "Yes."

"What were their names, the men?"

"Trimble—the breed's name was Harker and
they called the other one Kid."

"Trimble have another name?"

"Ralston, I think." She shook her head.

"Make us some food," Horsekiller said, strapping on a holster he had jerked off the older man's body.

The spent gunsmoke hung in the room and burned Hamp's eyes. He watched her wearily stand up and head for the cooking stove.

"When did they leave?" Hamp asked her.

She turned back and shrugged. "Middle of the afternoon."

"They say where they were going?"

"To collect a reward for her." She rattled the lids on the stove, opening them to stick in some split firewood.

"They say who was paying it?"

" 'Doom' was all I heard."

Hamp reloaded his Colt. "Was it Muldoone?"

She turned and frowned, put out at Horsekiller as he prowled around the cabin. Then she shook her head at Hamp. "I ain't sure."

She fried them some eggs, chopped up potatoes and fatback for them. It tasted all right to Hamp except for wadding up when he swallowed it. He'd hoped against the odds to find his wife, and soon. The two dead men on the floor did not bother him—they had lived and died by the gun. But besides his wife's abduction, he had all his money in a herd of steers grazing their way north toward Fort Smith.

"This your man?" Horsekiller pointed his fork at the younger one sprawled on the floor facedown.

She shook her head and stood wringing her hands.

"The old one?" He gave a head toss to the other one by the door.

"No. They bought me."

Horsekiller nodded and went on eating as if satisfied.

With an exhale, Hamp paused and considered her words. It was against the law to buy and sell anyone.

"Who sold you to them?" Hamp finally asked.

"Cotton Eye."

Hamp waited for Horsekiller to look up at him. "Who's he?"

"Mean sumbitch." The man went back to eating.

Damn, he was no closer to finding his wife and busy discovering lots of things. Junie, damnit, I'm coming.

Dawn came with some light rain. They wore slickers and rode west.

Chapter 11

"Where are they heading?" Hamp asked the Cherokee. The mist falling on his face soaked his beard stubble.

"Red River."

"Are there any more places they might stop over like the last one?"

Horsekiller nodded. "Plenty whiskey stores."

"You think they're headed for the next one?"

"Maybe Shorty's."

"You got a grudge against him too?"

"No. Shorty's run by white women. Shorty dead."

"Good," Hamp said, feeling clammy under his slicker.

The wet grass brushing his stirrups soaked his boots and socks. He wondered if this moisture went clear south into Texas and the hill country. The buttermilk sky overhead kept trailing a steady veil of moisture on them.

Horsekiller reined up at midday on a rise. He pointed to a bend in the river and a grove of trees. Some multicolored cattle and a few horses grazed nearby. "Shorty's."

"We just ride in?"

"They know you?"

"I never seen them before."

"We ride in."

"Suits me." Out of habit, he reached for the Colt's form under the raincoat and adjusted it.

Hamp blew his breath through his lips when he booted the bay off the hill. Was it asking too much that his Junie would be at this place? They could be riding into a setup—but a man had to die someday and he felt miserable enough to die if he couldn't have her back.

Four rain-slick horses stood hip-shot at the rack when they approached. Horsekiller nodded at them. No words needed to be spoken. Those mounts belonged to the kidnappers. Water dripped off the edge of the porch roof. No one was visible or standing outside. A yellow glare of candlelight inside shone in the small four-pane windows.

Horsekiller drew out the sawed-off shotgun he'd taken from the bootlegger's cabin. Hamp nodded in grave approval. This was no time for talking—each man knew what he must do.

They dismounted. The hair on the back of Hamp's neck felt stiff and an itch ran up his spine. He unbuttoned the raincoat standing close beside the horse, then loosened the girth. All the time, his muscles felt like a tightly wound spring about to explode. He took a moment to control his breathing. Then he nodded ready to Horsekiller and started up the steps.

His soggy boots at last on the rough-sawn boards under the porch roof, he shed the oilskin and put it over his left arm. Every muscle in his body tense, he readjusted the Colt, undid the hammer tie with his thumb, then reached for the door string.

When the door swung open, he could see the smoke-filled interior under the lamps. To the right was a rough bar, with three men in a row and a woman bartender who looked up and smiled.

"Welcome to Shorty's, mister." She was no young woman and she did a double take when Horsekiller moved to the left side of Hamp holding the scattergun at the ready.

"Hands high," Hamp ordered.

Things went to hell in a flash. A war cry came from the mouth of the breed. The tall one standing at the bar went for his gun and the shorter younger white man dove for the floor.

Hamp drew and fired at the tall one. The blast of Horsekiller's twelve-gauge was deafening indoors and then the sound of broken glass as the breed dove through it. The lights went out and they were submerged in darkness and silence.

"I give up," said the voice at Hamp's feet.

He reached down, found a collar and jerked the man up. "Don't try anything."

"'I won't, I swear."

"Where's my wife?"

"In the shed—out back."

"I'm lighting a lamp, is all," the woman bartender said.

"Good. You get that breed went out the window?" Hamp asked, seeing Horsekiller bent over the man on the floor.

"I didn't but he weighs more than he did. I got some buckshot in him. This one's going to die."

"Take me to find her," he said and shoved the Kid forward.

"Here, take a lamp," the woman said, producing another and setting it on the bar.

Hamp thanked her and holstered his Colt.

Horsekiller stood up. "I go see about the breed."

"Be careful. He may be more dangerous wounded than before."

They went out the back door into the drizzle. Mud sucked at Hamp's boots, squishing as they headed for an outbuilding. The Kid undid a bar and stepped over the threshold. Hamp held the lamp high to see the feed-grain-smelling room's contents.

Bound and gagged, she lay on the ground. The sight of her condition made the rage boil inside him. He handed the Kid the lamp.

"Try anything, you're dead." He reached for his jackknife as she blinked in disbelief at the sight of him.

The gag undone, she gasped for breath. "Oh, Hamp ."

"I'm here, baby. I'm here. They ain't going to hurt you anymore."

"Her all right?" Horsekiller asked from the doorway.

"I'm fine now," she said, with tears running down her cheeks, as she stripped away the ropes he had cut.

"Breed got away."

"Take the Kid back and tie him up. We'll be along." Hamp finished cutting her legs free.

On her knees, she threw her arms around him and plastered him with kisses. "My Gawd,

Hamp, I figured they'd sure killed you if you ever came along."

He pushed the hair back off her face and grinned at her. "Not on your life, woman."

"They hurt you?" he asked quietly.

"I'll live."

"No. I want to know."

She dropped her gaze. "Did they rape me?"

He nodded for her answer.

"Yes. They did."

In the next second he swept her up in his arms and held her tight. "I'm sorry. But I had to know. I love you, Junie, more than I ever dreamed I could any woman. And I've been coming—"

"I knew my cowboy was coming. I'm so glad you're all right."

Junie began to cry. Her tears soon soaked into his shirt as he tried to comfort her.

"Who was going to pay a reward for you?"

"Some woman in Texas, they said."

Muldoone? Damn her. "They never said her name?"

"I'm sorry, I never heard them say it."

He squeezed her tight—a grim image of Kathren Muldoone forced him to shut his eyes. *That bitch!*

*   *   *

The three rode away from Shorty's at daybreak. Horsekiller led the string of new horses. In the flannel light, a pair of boots twisted in the gentle wind under the great oak's canopy. Hamp never looked back. No law save in Fort Smith two hundred miles away, justice had been served.

Chapter 12

The slick-hided steers raised up with their mouths full of a twist of grass and looked with curiosity at the threesome as they approached the chuck wagon. Hamp was relieved to see Sam straighten up from his cooking and grin in disbelief at the sight of them.

"You went and done it!" he shouted and hurried to greet them.

Hamp dropped heavily to the ground and helped Junie off her horse, then turned to Sam and said, "We done it. How's things going?"

"Things going good here. 'Cept Clint's been gone over two days."

"Where was he going?" Hamp frowned at the news, wondering about his partner's absence that long from the herd with him away too. Not like him to do that.

"To check on something." Sam shook his head warily.

"Horsekiller, meet Sam Hayes."

"Glad to meet you."

"Tell me more about Clint," Hamp said as Junie finished hugging the cook.

"He rode out day before and we ain't seen hide nor hair of him since. And don't you worry none, ma'am, your wagon and black team is fine."

"Good." She nodded in approval at the cook.

"Bet you all are starved," Sam said, looking them over.

"We are."

"You need me to help you go look for him?" Horsekiller asked as Sam and Junie set out to feed them.

Hamp tried to put Clint's absence in perspective. His partner could handle himself in most cases, but no telling what held him up. Not like him to be gone that long when he was away from the herd as well.

Miguel rode in and smiled. "You brought her back?" He dismounted and stuck out his hand to Hamp and met Horsekiller too.

"How are the steers?"

"Getting fatter. They will look like pigs when

we get to Fort Smith." Miguel's broad smile of even white teeth sparkled in the sun.

"No trouble?" Hamp asked.

The youth shook his head. "I have been watching. There are some bad renegades in this part of the Nation."

"Yes, there are and it's also a great grass country to fill up these steers. I'm satisfied they'll be in good condition by the time we reach Fort Smith."

"Do we need to move them faster?" Miguel asked

"No, we have eight weeks and we can be up there in three. Ease them north a little each day to where they have fresh feed and water."

"What do you think happened to Clint?" Concern was written on the young man's brown face. He swept off his broad-brimmed straw hat and wiped his forehead on his sleeve.

"I have no idea. You and Sam will be in charge. Horsekiller is going with me tomorrow to look for him. Watch after Junie too while I am gone. Have everyone wear their guns."

"We will. I'm glad you found her." Miguel smiled and then, certain that the cook could not hear him, he said softly, "She makes better desserts than Sam."

"Don't tell him that." Hamp chuckled.

Dawn tried to peek through the low blanket of gray clouds that rolled in overnight. Most late-summer cloud formations built up in the afternoon into thundershowers. This was more like a winter-looking situation. Hamp saddled the roan horse from his string. Petey had pointed out to him the three horses with serious saddle sores that he was treating in the remuda.

"Tell them cowboys to use another saddle blanket. They must have narrow gulleted kack." Hamp shook his head in disapproval at the damage. Those ponies were out of service for the rest of the drive.

"I will," Petey said.

Hamp offered Horsekiller a fresh mount, but the Indian shook away his offer. The outlaws' horses they brought in were to be Horsekiller's pay. He planned to leave them with the trail herd until they returned.

Back at the wagon, Hamp stuffed some jerky and fried apple-raisin pies in his saddlebags. He kissed Junie good-bye and told her to stay close to Sam and keep her shotgun handy.

She gave him a concerned nod and he rode off with Horsekiller and his colt packhorse in tow. They used the ferry at Boggy Depot to cross the river. A white-whiskered older man who operated the rope ferry spoke about Clint going across two days before, but he had not seen hide nor hair of him since.

Hamp paid the man and they rode the road north. Not many shod horses in the Nation, so they could still see his imprints on the road. Plenty of rolling grassland with knots of post oak and some timber along the streams. The low clouds grew thicker and the temperature dropped.

Midmorning they caught up to another outfit headed north with a small herd of steers. Hamp estimated they had four to five hundred head of mixed-age cattle. Their animals looked gaunt and their hair had no gloss. They'd not sell them for much of a profit and with fall closing in the market for thin cattle was weak. No one wanted the expense of wintering them. Hamp was pleased they weren't his stock to worry about.

"Yeah," the redheaded Texas drover said, sitting a horse wearing a big B brand on its right hip. The man wound the rope up on the coil. "That feller came by here, spoke to us and rode on."

"Say anything about where to?"

"Nope. Said he had a herd behind going to Fort Smith was all."

Hamp knew the area well and thought about the Duffy place off to the west. Walsh Duffy made and sold whiskey when the U.S. marshals weren't looking, and kept some Indian doves at his outpost on Cherry Creek. Knowing Clint, he might have dropped by there for some cards, company, and whiskey. He turned to the Indian. "You know Duffy's place?"

Horsekiller nodded. "You want to check there?"

"Yeah, he might have gone there." It bewildered him why Clint had not come back by this time. That was unlike him. Unless he was being held against his will or, worse, had had an accident.

They short-loped a ways and then Horsekiller knew a shortcut. It was hardly a trail but wound through some post oaks and over a tall hill. Two hours later they came to the outpost and drew up their horses.

Still no sun and the clouds looked ready to pour rain. A surprising cool wind came on the eaves of it all. Their three horses snorted in the grass on the rise and caught their breath as the riders studied the ramshackle outfit. Hamp handed a fried pie from his saddlebags to Horsekiller.

"You ain't got a war going with Duffy, have you?" Hamp asked, recalling their stopover at another outpost.

Horsekiller shook his head. "No, but I know him good."

After eating their pies, they wiped their mouths on their sleeves, picked up their reins and advanced on the outpost. In the stacked-pole corrals, a big strawberry roan lifted his head and nickered at Hamp's pony.

"He knows us?" Horsekiller asked, tossing his head toward the horse.

"Yes. Clint calls him Jude."

Horsekiller nodded. "Maybe your friend is here?"

The first drops of rain began to penetrate the fabric of his shirt. Hamp checked the loads in his Colt. "Maybe."

Chapter 13

Walsh Duffy was a big man with a wavy gray beard. He wore his faded shirt open at the throat and his bushy chest hair spilled out of it. He waddled rather than walked over behind his makeshift bar set on barrels and nodded solemnly at them.

"What'll it be, gents?" His deep-set eyes looked hard until he recognized the Cherokee. "Ah, Horsekiller, who's your sidekick?"

"The man who wants to know about the strawberry roan in the corral," Hamp said flatly.

"I've got a bill of sale from his owner." Duffy held his hands high to demonstrate he was doing nothing but going for that paper. He opened a green tin box and turned with paper in his hand. "Here."

Hamp stepped forward with a look around to be sure there were no tricks and no one else in the place. Then with his left hand he shook the folded paper open and pressed it on the bar.

> Roan gelding, seven years old, wire scar left fetlock. Branded with WC on his left shoulder. I do hereby sell this horse and transfer title to which was blank, signed X.

"Who the hell is X?" Hamp met the big man's gaze.

"Charlie Seasons. He can't write." Duffy's great hands were pressed flat on the rough board surface.

"That horse belongs to my partner, Clint Barton, who hasn't been seen in three days or so."

"What's this Barton look like?"

"Tall Texan. Burly built, leans forward when he speaks to you. Blond hair and blue eyes."

"He's been in here before, but,"—Duffy shook his head—" he ain't been in here anytime lately."

"Seasons say where he got that horse?"

Duffy shook his head. "I gave him twenty for the roan."

"That was a bargain."

"You don't ask lots of questions down here and live very long."

Hamp considered the man's words as if they

were either a warning or advice for him. "I'm still looking for my partner. He must have met foul play to lose his horse."

"Not here, he didn't."

Still upset with the matter, Hamp turned to Horsekiller. "You know this Seasons?"

Horsekiller nodded matter-of-factly. "You buying whiskey?"

Hamp nodded he would, deeply engrossed in his concerns. Maybe some rotgut whiskey might help him too. He sure had no answers for Clint's disappearance. If this Seasons had bush-whacked him, he might never have an answer.

"Pour us some," he said and dug in his vest pocket for a few coins.

Horsekiller put the hat on the back of his head and grinned. "Thought you were going to talk all day."

Bottle in his hand, Duffy laughed. "You two going after Seasons?"

"I need some answers." Hamp considered the brown liquid in the dim light of the grubby sa-loon. Possum and coon hides hung from the rafters and some deer hides were piled on a rack. Stiff cow hides made a large stack.

"You buy hides?"

"I take 'em all in trade. Ain't much else to do around here. They skin out cattle that die on the trail. It's mostly Injun women do that so they can get some food. Some men trap and tree the others." Duffy shook his head. "Just plain country around here, not rich, and Parker's damn marshals come around all the time to try to put me out of business. Ain't supposed to be any firewater in the Nation. Hell, a man would die without it."

Hamp nodded he heard him. It wasn't bad whiskey, but listening to the patter on the cedar roof shingles, he wished the rain had waited.

"I'll give you your money back for the roan," he finally said to the bar man.

"Fair enough. Woman's got some stew and cornbread ready to go. Have a seat." Over his shoulder he called out their food order.

Horsekiller was already bobbing his head to say he was ready for it. So they took seats at the bench with their backs to the wall, removed their hats and waited for the Indian woman of ample proportions to appear in the doorway of the lean-to with two heaping bowls of steaming stew.

"Good thing we stopped here," Horsekiller said, ready to dig in. "That last pie was a small one."

They slept the night in one of Duffy's horse sheds that sheltered a haystack. Hamp woke up to the dripping dawn, but the rain was past. He felt stiff and ready to get back to the herd as soon as they found Clint or his remains. More and more he wondered if remains might be all that was left of his partner. Clint lived hard and he would have died the same way.

After one more of her meals, they rode west. Horsekiller thought he knew where they'd find Seasons if he was home. The wet brush soaked into Hamp's pants legs. He didn't want to be encumbered with his chaps if hell broke loose, so they rode hung over the horn. Horsekiller led the roan and his packhorse. The way was less than a wagon road and they went uphill all the time. Hamp could look off at times when the trail swung out on a point and see the fields and grassy open bottom country far beneath them.

They crossed over a ridge finally and began a descent. Hamp wondered if this Seasons place was at the end of the world. Then he spotted a thin veil of smoke coming from under the green umbrella that covered the sea of large timber below them.

"That's Seasons'," Horsekiller said. "He will think we are Parker's men."

"What will he do?"

"Run away."

"Which way?"

"Over the mountain, I think."

"What should we do?"

"Hobble these two horses. I will ride around and try to stop him. You go on down, slow like, and be plenty careful."

"You do the same. Two shots means come on the run."

Horsekiller agreed and both dismounted. This was the first time Hamp recalled the Cherokee ever acting in a hurry. Amused at the man's sudden swiftness, he kept his thoughts to himself as they each took an animal to secure. After hobbling them, both men straightened.

"Go ahead," Hamp told him. At his words, Horsekiller jumped on his horse and rode south, spanking his pony to hurry. He soon disappeared in the trees.

Hamp checked his cinch, swung up, then shifted the Colt on his hip in readiness and took the trail downhill. A musky smell of rotten leaves hung in the humid forest air. Two white-tail does lifted their heads to scent him, turned with a fury and raced away. Little sunlight found the ground under the thick canopy of leaves. Squirrels scolded him overhead and crows cawed.

In an hour he could smell the smoke and soon saw the small, crude cabin. He made the decision to dismount and make his way forward using the great tree trunks for shields. He paused, but could not make out any activity around the cabin. He moved closer with his gun in hand.

Then the sharp report of a rifle and a bullet slapped the tree a few feet above his head. He dropped to his knees and studied where the puff of smoke had come from—a window in the cabin. Good thing they weren't an accurate shot, he decided with his back pressed against a rough trunk. The range too great for his pistol, he considered his other options. Another report of the rifle went whining off through the forest.

At that moment, he would have given a big price for the .44/40 in Sam's wagon back at the herd. No time for regrets. Time for patience on his part. Had Seasons gone over the mountain before he got there or was he the shooter?

Hamp heard a horse coming from the south off the mountain. He couldn't make out the rider until the familiar unblocked hat of Horsekiller appeared. The Cherokee rode up beside the house, reined his horse up and shouted something Hamp could not understand. Indian words, no doubt.

Someone soon appeared in the door with a gun. It was not a man. The short individual looked very rejected. It was a girl, Hamp decided, watching Horsekiller dismount and take away her weapon. He holstered his Colt and headed there.

"They already left," Horsekiller said, with a toss of his head toward the direction he came from.

"Who?"

"Her man Seasons and a tough breed called Ira McKay."

"They got much of a head start?"

"Couple of hours."

Hamp looked hard at the young girl who'd shot at him. She looked crestfallen.

"You know where they went?" Hamp asked her.

Horsekiller repeated the question in his language. She shook her head. He jerked her up and talked tougher to her.

"Green!" she stammered out.

"Where?" Hamp asked him.

"Green Town."

"Far away?"

Horsekiller shook his head, continuing to talk to the girl like an angry parent. Hamp went back for his horse. Mounted, he rode down the trail for the roan and the colt. When he returned,

Horsekiller met him and offered a shortcut up the hillside.

"How does this McKay fit in?"

"He is the number one bad one in the Nation. Robs the old people of their money." Horsekiller's eagle feather shook as he spoke about the renegade. "He rapes little girl seven. If you can do something, anything bad or despicable, he does so for his own laughs."

"Bad enough guy. Who was that girl back there?" Hamp asked over his shoulder as their horses cat-hopped up the mountain.

"My granddaughter."

Chapter 14

Green Town, a jumble of shacks bathed in the
fire of sundown, did not impress Hamp. He felt
guilty over being away so long from his wife and
the herd, but still, he needed to find Clint if there
was even a chance he was alive. He rode beside
Horsekiller, who carried the trapdoor rifle over
his lap.

"You think he's here?" Hamp disliked the
cold looks at them from the women who were
cooking in pots in front of their shacks.

Horsekiller dropped down off his horse and
nodded. "I will go in this place. If Seasons or
McKay is here, we will know."

"Wait. If he's in there he's going to try to
shoot you. I'm coming too."

The Cherokee scowled in disapproval but
waited. Hamp hitched his horse to the wheel of

an empty wagon, shifted his holster, then followed his scout.

The door was an old hide. Horsekiller swept
it back. The room's darkness was lighted by
some smoky candles. Hamp felt his stomach
tighten, but he slipped in to stand beside
Horsekiller, who was spouting orders in Cherokee. His eyes started to adjust to the room's poor
light, then the light went out.

The trapdoor rifle's blast hurt Hamp's ears,
but the blinding gunsmoke set everyone to
choking and seeking escape. Hamp swept past
the stinking hide to get out of the bad smoke
and ended up bent over coughing, with his
shoulder against the log sides. Tears blurred his
vision when he tried to find the old man.

Was he still inside? Then he heard Horsekiller
cursing. Next the Cherokee came around the
building with the rifle in one hand and a boy by
the collar in the other.

"Who's he?"

"Him Rudy Brown Dog. Tell him what you
know about that roan horse."

The Indian youth shook his head. Horsekiller
raised him off the ground by his handful of shirt
collar. Whatever he said in Cherokee must have
been enough.

"They tried to rob him. He was mad and went

for his gun. They shot him, but he get away in the bushes. So they get scared, took his horse and ran."

"Who tried to rob him?"

"Ah—" But a growl from Horsekiller forced him to spit it out. "McKay was the leader. Seasons was there, and some more. I don't know them. I swear."

"Where did they do this?" Damn, his partner might be dead out there in the brush.

"Somewhere on Stone Creek—" The youth held out his hands as if uncertain about the exact location. "I wasn't there or I'd tell you."

Hamp stood in the growing darkness and looked at Horsekiller. "Were they in there?"

"I think they had left before we got here, but I saw this rat and caught him."

"You did good, Horsekiller. How far is this Stone Creek?"

"Many hours ride."

"We need to head there." He looked around in the growing darkness. "What are we going to do with him?"

"Maybe cut him."

"No!" The youth's voice grew high-pitched as he struggled in the old man's grasp.

Horsekiller nodded. "You understand English good enough. You ever get into something like this again I come back and slice off your whole thing. Understand?"

"Me do! Me do!"

"Get out of here." He gave the scrawny youth a hard shove and he just about fell down in his panic to run away. Ignoring Brown Dog's flight pell-mell down the wagon tracks, Horsekiller headed for a woman busy cooking across the street.

"We want to buy some supper."

She smiled at the words and hurried with her skirt in her hand for the crude shelter. In seconds she returned with two chipped bowls and spoons. Then like a sergeant in charge, she began filling each bowl for them.

"You eat," she said, motioning for Hamp to come closer and take his dish.

After they finished, Hamp paid her fifty cents and she impulsively hugged him. "You be careful. Me have food anytime you hungry. Come back soon," she chattered after them, doing lots of head bobbing with Horsekiller.

They rode southwest under the stars, the colt showing the weariness of the long haul, so in the darkness Hamp stopped, switched the pack saddle and the load to the roan.

"I can leave him with someone," Horsekiller said, referring to the colt.

"Be a good idea." Hamp had been watching the flicker of lightning on the western horizon. The storm was still distant enough, but he could hear the low grumble of thunder.

"It may rain too," Horsekiller said.

They mounted up and rode on, reaching a better road to head south. In the next hour the thunder grew even closer and Hamp began looking for some shelter like an empty cabin or shed in the inky world they passed through.

"There's a shed," he said in a flash of lightning overhead.

The storm was within a mile of them. Horsekiller agreed and they rode for it. Once under the structure's roof, they loosened cinches just as the rain began to beat down. Blasts of blinding light and ear-shattering roars were everywhere. Four horses and two men filled the dirt-floored building.

The shakes began to leak under the downpour, but most were drips. Hamp put on his slicker and found a corner to squat in. A bolt struck a nearby tree and big limbs crashed to the ground. He felt grateful they were in the building, but he knew the hard rain would remove any of Clint's tracks they might have been able to find.

When the rain had passed, they hobbled their

horses and grabbed a few hours of shut-eye. Without any coffee, they ate the last pies and mounted up. They reached a sleepy village in a few hours. Horsekiller gave a woman two dollars to keep his colt and they asked her about seeing Clint. She shook her head.

"You have coffee?" Hamp asked. His teeth were about to float away from the lack of caffeine.

"Sure," she beamed and he nodded in approval at Horsekiller.

"Got fry bread too."

"We'll take it," Hamp said and his tracker smiled.

Her coffee proved to be more chicory than coffee, but her delicious fry bread made up for it. In a half hour they were moving on. Rock Creek wandered out of the hills to the east. Dense brush grew along the banks, and the water was running brown and fresh from the rain the night before.

When Hamp spotted the buzzards, his heart stopped. Must have been two dozen, in a great spiral riding the up currents. Horsekiller nodded and they set spurs to their horses. To get to them meant crossing the creek, so Hamp looked for a shallow ford, but in the end sent his horse into the muddy water. He struck bottom and finally his horse clambered out the far side.

He pushed through the willows and immediately saw the skinned cow carcass with half a dozen vultures bouncing around her taking their fill. Settled back in the saddle, he looked skyward and thanked the powers above it wasn't Clint. What to do next?

"We can go ask some people around here if they saw him," Horsekiller said, as if reading his mind when he rode up beside him on his dripping-wet horse.

"Good idea."

They recrossed the creek and started up the road. Horsekiller talked to a man who was busy gathering his corn in a field with his wife and children. He nodded when Horsekiller asked him if he had seen someone riding the roan horse a few days before.

"Drover. He came by here."

Hamp heard the man's words and wondered what Clint was doing in this country. The herd was a long way from here. He shook his head in bewilderment listening to Horsekiller continue to talk to the man.

"You see Quin McKay up here?" Horsekiller asked.

The man shook his head and turned back to

his task of shucking corn. He looked hard as he waded in the dry stalks to twist off the ears. His wife spoke sharply to the children in a guttural language. Their dark eyes quickly turned away and they too went to work, bouncing ears off the wagon's wooden sides.

Horsekiller mounted up and gave a toss of his unblocked hat eastward. When they were beyond the family's hearing he shook his head.

"McKay has these people afraid to talk about him."

"I wondered what was wrong when he wouldn't talk to you anymore."

Two Indian women were coming down the road driving a wagon. Their team consisted of two spindly young horses. Hamp could smell the green hides that they had piled in the bed. One was an older woman, the other an attractive-looking woman in her twenties.

"We are looking for a white man," Horsekiller explained.

The two women looked at each other and then turned back.

"He may have been shot."

The women acted like they could not understand him. Horsekiller spoke to them in his language.

They shook their heads and looked worried about something.

"Must be Creek," he said. Then he made sign language and they acted even more upset.

Not expecting him to get much out of the pair, Hamp rode on, curious to look at the wagon's contents. Several stiff hides were piled in there. Then the younger woman gathered her skirt and stepped around the spring seat and into the wagon box.

She lifted up some hides and motioned for Hamp to come closer. "Is this who you look for?"

He blinked in disbelief at the pale face of Clint Barton lying in a nest of blankets.

Chapter 15

"Where's the closest doctor?" Hamp asked the woman.

She shook her head. Obviously she didn't know of one.

"Where were you taking him?"

"To woman who we hoped could help him," she said, with a concerned look on her coffee-colored face.

"'Becca—" Clint said in a rasping whisper that knifed Hamp's heart.

"Clint, can you hear me?" Hamp asked, stepping off his horse and into the wagon bed to kneel beside him.

Behind the bristle of whiskers, Clint's blanched skin under his tan looked too pale. His usually blue eyes looked fuzzy as he tried to focus on Hamp. His lips were dried and cracked when he moved them to speak. "Yeah. I hear you, pard."

"We'll get you some medical care." Hamp couldn't see the wound or wounds, but knew his partner had suffered a lot of trauma. He could only hope he wasn't too late to save him.

Clint nodded and closed his eyes.

Hamp rose, watching the woman tenderly replace the covers over his partner.

"This woman?" he asked, concerned about the best medical attention they could get for him.

Concern written on her face, she nodded. "The best I know. But you know that McKay is looking for him."

"McKay don't scare us. How far away is this woman?" he asked, stepping off the wagon to remount his horse.

"A few miles."

"Let's get him there."

She agreed, stepped back in place at the seat after another look at her patient. Then, taking up the reins, she made the thin horses trot.

"You know about this woman she speaks about?" he asked Horsekiller, riding his horse close to the Indian's mount.

"Name's Mary Drake. The old woman says she's very good."

"I just hope she is and we ain't too late. He looks tough." He twisted in the saddle. Obviously this outlaw McKay had the two women worried that he might hurt them for tending to Clint. The post oak–clad hills around them could hold any enemy. He shifted the Colt and wished for the rifle at the chuck wagon.

The wagon tracks wound through the cured grass down a gentle valley that followed the creek's brush-choked course. Anywhere there could be an ambush. But he wanted someone with experience at doctoring working on his partner.

The team showed signs of weakening and stumbling when Rebecca pointed at the farmstead ahead. Hamp nodded and looked about. No sign of any pursuit. He settled in the saddle, wondering if this was the best choice. Her team would never make it much further, for sure.

"There's a doctor at Patches," Horsekiller said. "But I don't know how good he is."

"How far is that?"

"Twenty miles."

Hamp shook his head, concerned about the distance. "I don't think he can take a lot more hauling."

Horsekiller nodded that he understood.

The house was paintless, and chickens scattered before the team when she drew up at the porchless front. A straight-backed small woman came to the door, drying her hands.

"What's wrong?" she asked, after blinking at the lathered team. Her gray hair pulled tight in a bun, she was a half-breed and moved on the balls of her feet.

"A man who is shot," Rebecca said and climbed in back.

"Who shot him?" she asked, climbing on the wheel to look in the box.

"McKay and his men."

"Lucky they didn't kill him. You two carry him inside," Mary ordered as if accustomed to telling people what to do.

Hamp nodded to Horsekiller and climbed in the wagon. Rebecca helped move the moaning Clint to the tailgate, then Hamp jumped down and the two of them carried the wounded man to the house.

Hamp could see the bandage on his upper left leg.

"Bullet still in him?" he asked Rebecca.

She nodded. "I could not dig it out."

"When did this happen?" Mary asked, walking beside them and ushering them in the open front door.

"Three days ago. I was afraid that McKay's

men were still around and would kill him," the girl said, looking with concern at her patient.

"He say why they shot him?" Hamp asked, crossing the threshold into the woman's house.

"He said they tried to rob him in the night after he left a card game." Rebecca moved aside to let the two men put Clint on the clean sheet. "He went for his gun and they shot him. He fell off his horse and ran into the bushes. When they chased him, he thinks he wounded two of them and they rode away. He must have crawled three miles to our place."

"Thanks."

"We were afraid you were with McKay when you first stopped us," she said.

Hamp nodded that he understood, busy watching Mary cut away the filthy pants with scissors and expose Clint's white leg. She tossed the scraps on the floor and Rebecca began to gather them. Then Mary cut the bandage and exposed the purple bruised thigh and the black crusted hole the size of the end of his finger.

"We must get the bullet out," Mary said. "Get that piece of leather for him to bite on and everyone help hold him down."

"No whiskey?" Horsekiller asked.

Mary shook her head with a frown.

"I'll get some from my horse." The Indian disappeared out the front door and soon was back with a pint.

They raised Clint's head up and he sipped from the neck of the brown bottle. When he had drunk a little, they laid him down and inserted the piece of flat rawhide in his mouth.

Mary returned with some clean shiny tools in a washbasin and set them down on the night-stand. Then she washed her hands thoroughly and dried them on a snow-white sack towel. She nodded at the three of them to take their places.

"Sorry, but this will hurt," Mary said to Clint and motioned for the others to hold him down.

Hamp and Horsekiller had a leg apiece to hold at the shin, Rebecca held down his upper torso. At Mary's first probe, Clint hollered through his teeth, but the surgeon never looked up, intent on recovering the slug.

Hamp watched her expertise. He knew the gouging was necessary despite his partner's protest through his clamped mouth. It took all of Hamp's strength to contain the leg she worked upon. Time slipped by slowly and the job looked endless until she exclaimed, "Got it!" and held up the bloody object in her fingers.

"Empty some cartridges. We need some gun-powder," Mary said, looking down as fresh blood spilled out of the hole.

Hamp used the drawer on her dresser to pry the lead off and poured the powder in a small dish. When he and Horsekiller had unloaded about ten bullets each in the glass container she nodded in approval and took the dish.

"We don't have much time. When I get it packed in the wound, someone must touch it off with a lighted match before it gets too blood-soaked. You men must hold him down and look away. It will flash bright."

Hamp handed Rebecca several matches from his vest. She shared a glum nod with him over what she must do. Hamp pressed down on Clint's shoulders, the Indian on his feet.

Mary swabbed out the wound seeping fresh blood, then she poured the grainy black dust into the hole. "Now!"

She turned aside as Rebecca struck the match head and it flamed into an orange fire. When she touched off the powder, the blast was blinding, even with Hamp's eyes closed. The sulfurous stench filled the room with a cloud of smoke and Clint screamed in pain, forced to stay there by his partner's best efforts.

Clint fainted and Mary waved a towel to clear the smoky air in the room.

"What now?" Hamp asked.

"It's up to him," Mary said.

And God, Hamp decided. He closed his eyes. The fumes were burning them. Rebecca was opening doors and windows to get fresh air inside. Hamp looked down at Clint's beard-stubbled face and wondered if his partner had the strength to survive. Either way McKay would pay for this.

Chapter 16

About sundown, he left Horsekiller to guard his partner and rode for the herd. It was past time that he got back and checked on Junie and the crew. Miguel and Sam could handle most anything, but he still did not feel right with both bosses being gone this long. He knew he must find the Foggy Bottoms Road if he was ever going to find them. He headed southwest in the bloody orange sunset.

Dark overtook him and an old man at a crossroads store gave him new directions: to ride west on the wagon road in front of his business until he came to the more used north-south Texas Road in about ten miles, then turn south on it.

With stars for his ceiling, he rode through the timbered darkness and out then in the open rolling sea and back into the inky night, but the horse held a trot and he knew he would be fine for many more miles. Before dawn first grayed the eastern sky he was headed south and crossed the ferry an hour past sunup.

"Find your man?" the operator asked, reeling them across the brown water.

Hamp nodded. "Shot up, but he's in good hands."

"I told you he never came back," the old man said and punctuated it with brown spit over the side, never missing a stroke with his sinewy arms on the reel handle.

"Thanks."

"Who shot him?"

"An outlaw named McKay."

"Bad hombre. The Fort Smith marshal's been down here looking for him. You know he raped a woman over by Hanover."

Hamp shook his head. "No, but I understand he's tough."

"Them deputies will tree him soon. They always get their man."

Hamp agreed, hoping they found him soon. He paid the ferryman when they docked, and then he rode on. By midafternoon, he spotted the familiar yellow canvas top on a high hill with the letters B BAR M painted in black on the side. He forced the weary horse to lope and saw

Sam reining up the mules at his approach. Then Junie drove up behind him and even at the distance he could see the excitement on her face. Good he'd be back with her in moments. Perhaps all was well with the herd. He hoped so.

"Going good?" he asked the whiskered Sam on the spring seat.

"Yeah. Did you find Clint?"

"Yeah. He's been shot up, but he should live."

"Hamp! Hamp!" Junie cried, running through the tall twisted grass with her arms out for him. It knifed his guts that he'd been away from her so long.

"How is he?" she asked with her face against him.

"Fine. How are you?" With her fingers she lifted the windswept long hair from her face. "With you back, I'm fine."

"How is Miguel?" He looked to the sea of cattle coming over the rise, scattered out, snatching mouthsful as they came.

"Upset. He thinks they stole ten head last night."

"Who did it?"

"Rustlers. He wasn't sure."

Hamp looked to the south. The young man's familiar sombrero was not in sight. "He didn't go after them, did he?"

"No. I told him to wait for you."

"Good." Hamp still did not see his main man, but he might be on the fringe of the drive.

"When did you eat last?" she demanded.

"I don't remember." He was still looking for Miguel.

She frowned and pounded his chest with the side of her fist to get his attention. "Let's go to Sam's wagon. He has some food, I'm sure."

"Okay," he said and hugged her for her concerns about his welfare—a new side to her that made him feel important for the moment. Important to her, anyway. He took her hand and led the horse. Her team was grazing and looked in no threat to leave. Some food might be good, as drained as he felt.

"Señor Hamp!"

He turned and saw the familiar sombrero of his man as he pushed his pony through the thick grass. Junie squeezed his hand with a there-I-told-you grip.

"I'll go see about some food for you."

Hamp agreed. "Miguel, what's happening?"

"Oh, *patrón*, they have been stealing some cattle."

"Starving Indians?"

"No, I would give them a cripple one."

Hamp nodded—they never denied begging Indians a head or two.

"They cut them out and drove them to the west. They had unshod horses, but few people have shod horses in the Nation."

"First you've missed?"

"Sí. We haven't bunched them up close at night because they were coming back in the herd and they are so fat they are gentle."

"Good. I'll get some food and we'll go see what we can find out. You can show me the tracks. Get me a fresh horse while I eat."

"Sí."

"You should sleep a few hours," Junie said under her breath.

"I can sleep tonight."

'Did you sleep last night?"

"No." He shook his head to dismiss her concerns and not hurt her feelings.

"That's why you should sleep some now," she insisted, struggling to keep up with him in the thick grass.

"I will later. Hello, Sam."

"Well, good to see you." The cook swung down from his spring seat and then stood straddle-legged to make his canvas pants more comfortable. "You find Clint?"

"I did. He's shot up, but he may make it. Miguel says they ran off ten head."

Sam shook his whiskered face. "Been job enough for us to keep them together, let alone chase down rustlers. I told him we better all stay here until you all got back." Then he nodded as Junie came from the back with several biscuits for him. "Is Clint bad off?"

"He was shot and had to crawl for some help. You ever hear him talk about Rebecca?"

Sam shook his head. "Who's she?"

"Indian woman who's tried to save his life."

"Clint has lots of lady friends." Sam smiled with a smirk.

Hamp agreed with a nod. "I left Horsekiller to watch him. This McKay and his gang have everyone afraid. Must be a bad breed."

Hamp took his first bite. "Break out one of those rifles, Sam. I aim to go find them rustlers."

"You're going to take Miguel along?" Junie asked

"You better," Sam said.

Deep in consideration, Hamp chewed on the bread, listening to his wife's lament about how they didn't have any cooked food for him. He shook his head to dismiss her concerns. "I'll be fine."

Miguel brought up the fresh horse.

"Get a rifle for each of us," Hamp said, and his cowboy nodded.

"Come back to me," she said and then impulsively kissed him on the cheek.

He put two biscuits in his vest pockets and took some jerky strips from Sam. Then he finished his last mouthful and headed for the water barrel. "We'll be back."

He drank a dipper full and then hung up the metal dispenser. "You don't worry," he said to Junie. With a sweep of his arm he hugged her, then lightly kissed her forehead.

"Better go."

She nodded and he caught the horse's reins. When he swung up, Miguel handed him a Winchester. Sam stuffed a box of cartridges in his saddlebags.

"You two keep your heads down," Sam said and then spat tobacco to the side.

"You two do the same," Hamp said and they hurried off.

Miguel showed him the tracks and it wasn't hard to follow the prints. The rustlers made no effort to hide them, and that worried Hamp. They were either stupid or bold. Fresh plops were obvious and the prints showed the stock had been walking, not driven hard.

"Better keep an eye out. This may be an ambush," Hamp said, standing in the saddle. His entire body felt stiff from the long hours in the saddle.

"I see some buzzards." Miguel pointed to the southwest at the circling black specks in the sky.

Hamp agreed. "That may be where they're butchering them. Let's ride."

They reined up when it was obvious the buzzards' interest was over the next rise. The horses left tied to some brush, they crept up the grassy knoll and soon peered down on the homestead. There was cooking going on judging from the smoke coming from a grove of trees. A bloody carcass hung on a makeshift scaffold. Several men sat around and some Indian women were busy scurrying around camp.

"Some are white men," Miguel said, looking from where they laid belly down in the grass.

"How many of them do you count?"

"Four, maybe five, counting a boy."

"They look to me to be drinking."

"Yeah, they are celebrating. I guess they think they got away with the cattle."

Hamp nodded and began backing off for the horses. "Let's get out the rifles. I aim to get the rest of them back before they butcher 'em."

The Winchester loaded to the gate, he nodded to Miguel. They swung up and took a course around the hill so they would be close when they were first seen by the thieves. On the way, they crossed a small stream and pushed up the bank, then used the cover of some brush.

"Ready?" Hamp asked.

Miguel nodded and they rode stirrup to stir-rup.

"When we get around those last trees, get ready for hell to break loose."

"I understand."

"Let's ride." Hamp stood up in the stirrups and aimed the rifle over the heads of the men. The rifle cracked and he had to check his upset mount.

The men looked wide-eyed and began to scramble.

"Hands in the air or die," Hamp shouted.

One of the men took off running for a shed. Miguel spurred his horse after him. Two stood up, hands in the air, and the third one tried to pull a handgun out of his belt.

Hamp reined up the bay horse and snapped off a shot at him. The impact of the bullet spun the man around and he crumpled in a pile. Hamp turned and saw Miguel coming back driving a youth of perhaps eighteen ahead of his horse.

"Get over there," Hamp ordered. "Who the hell are you?"

"Gunthers," the older man with the beard said.

"Where I come from we hang cattle rustlers."

"By Gawd, a man's got to eat."

"Taking ten head ain't for just eating. Miguel, tie their hands up."

All the while, Hamp wondered about the women, who had fled for cover at the first shot. Neither he nor Miguel needed hot lead in the back. His helper soon had their hands bound and Hamp bent over to examine the shot one. He wouldn't need any medical help—dead.

"Get them steers headed back," Hamp said to his man. "I'll cover them."

"What ya going to do with us?"

"I should hang you, but I don't have time. You ever again steal any B Bar M cattle I'll shoot you no questions asked and let them buzzards up there eat ya."

The three looked relieved. He could see the nervous Indian women peering at him from beyond the shacks and watching his partner herding the steers out of the makeshift corral and onto the wagon tracks. It would be long past dark before they were back with the herd.

Chapter 17

The midday heat and humidity woke Hamp in a thick sweat. Despite the growing wind and noisy birds in the trees, he had slept several hours, lying on his blankets. His eyes felt like burning firepits as he tried to focus them on the tramped-down grass about the camp. Sam's wagon was across from where he had slept under a great oak tree. His wife's lighter one was to his right.

She came on the run from Sam's fly shade when she noticed he was awake. He smiled, pleased at the sight of her, and yawned hard. If it hadn't turned so hot he'd've slept into the next day. In the distance he could hear the cattle bawling to each other in the communication form of settled stock.

"You hungry?" she asked.

"I could eat."

"Good. I've got some stew cooking. Did you have any trouble?"

He shook his head. "We only lost one head."

"Who were they?"

"Some worthless trash. You doing all right?" He used some effort to get to his feet.

"Fine."

"We better take your wagon and go get Clint today. He should be able to travel—'less he took a turn for the worse."

"Good. I'd love to see the country."

"It's like here, rolling grassy hills."

"Oh, I just like to be with you."

He nodded that he understood. An arm over her shoulder, he kissed her on the cheek. "I forget sometimes."

"Forget me?" She looked up into his face.

"No, I forget what a husband's supposed to do."

She laughed softly. "No, Hamp, you're a good husband. Land sakes, with all you've got to think about and all that's happened. I'm just glad to be part of your life."

"Glad to have you along too. How's it going, Sam?"

The cook had some coffee poured and handed him the metal cup. "Not bad," he said. "Your Missus may put me out of work."

"No—" she protested.

"I was just kidding. Been dang nice having her along to help." He smiled behind his beard like a mischievous devil. "What about Clint?"

"I'm going after him. Horsekiller and a woman named Rebecca are with him."

Junie delivered him a plate of food and he took it with a nod of gratitude.

"Cattle are doing wonderful," Sam said. "They'll be fatter than a Christmas goose time we need to drive them up there."

Hamp agreed between bites of the flavorful food. "That's what sells them."

After he ate, he and Sam hitched the team to Junie's rig. With her beside him, he set out for his partner, filled with mixed feelings of worry and concern about whether Clint had even survived the gunshot and the tough treatment for his wound. The wind had come up and swept the grass tops like a sea of water in waves.

They drove down the last grade in late afternoon. The familiar sight of Horsekiller's unblocked hat sitting in a chair by Mary's front door told him things were under control.

"How's he doing?" he asked the Indian, tying off the reins and ready to climb down.

"Pretty good."

The words made him feel better. "He able to travel, you reckon?"

Horsekiller nodded and drew a deep breath up his nose.

"What else is wrong?"

"I think McKay is getting some men together to come over here and do him in. Mary heard that word when she went to help a woman birth a baby."

Hamp looked around. Nothing looked out of place. He turned back to Horsekiller. "When do you expect them?"

The Cherokee shrugged his narrow shoulders under the worn shirt. "When they come."

"We better wait till morning to try to move him," Hamp said, seeing his wife talking to Rebecca and then going inside.

Horsekiller agreed.

He saw Junie on her knees in the shadowy room beside the bed. Clint's hand clutched hers as she spoke softly to him.

"How are you?" he asked the whiskered, pale patient.

"Better," Clint managed in a coarse voice. "Damn, you've got a pretty wife."

"I think you're going to live." Hamp laughed aloud. He knew Clint still was not recovered or he wouldn't be lying there in bed.

In late evening past sundown, with the locust sizzling in the trees around the place, Hamp sat on the front stoop talking with Horsekiller.

"I better go home," the older man said. "Now you can watch him."

"How much do I owe you?"

"You never mentioned money."

"You've been working for me for several weeks."

"I been eating good. I'll come or send for those horses you gave me."

"Hey, I appreciate all you've done for me and looking after him in there."

"You ain't seen no sign of that breed McKay around your herd, have you?" Horsekiller's black eyes narrowed with the serious tone of his voice.

"No, but I have all the Mexican boys armed at the herd."

"I want to warn you he's spiteful. It will eat at his guts when he learns he didn't kill your partner." Horsekiller shook his hat and the eagle feather on it rattled.

"You hear anything, let me know. We ain't due up there at Fort Smith for four more weeks. We can make the drive from here in a week or so. I hate to push on because we might not find this much good grass."

"I know what you mean. Just be careful."

"I'll have to be." Hamp bobbed his head, his face filled with concern. "I'm afraid Clint's going to laid up for a while longer."

"He'll make it."

"But not fast."

Horsekiller nodded.

Hamp held up some folding money from his vest pocket to the light from the doorway behind them and counted out thirty dollars. "Here, buy you some beans."

"Thanks. It's too much for an old man's short time working for you. But I will listen for any word on that little bastard."

"What's McKay's story?"

"Father ran a trading post store. He was an older man and this Cherokee girl moved in with him because he was rich and she wanted all the goods in his store for herself. Her foolishness only got her hard work, many beatings for being lazy and that redheaded bastard in her belly. Her name was Cane Reed. When she learned that McKay only wanted her to work hard, then rut her body every night and have her bear his seed, she ran off with an outlaw, Billy Buckboard, to the Kiamichi Mountains.

"She lived with his gang and McKay grew up among them, so he learned early. One day, the U.S. marshals from Fort Smith came and arrested Buckboard for robbing a small post office and killing the postmaster. Judge Parker hung him for that.

"Cane Reed was drunk one day. She fell off a horse and hit her head on a rock and died. Her son was maybe nine and then he had no one. When he was fifteen he rode up to his father's store to claim his inheritance. They had a terrible bloody fight. Cut each other up with knives. McKay crawled off when it was over and some Indian women treated him for months.

"The old man sold out his store meanwhile and went to Fort Smith for health reasons.

"Then McKay shot a man in a drunken brawl over cards at Tahlequah. The Cherokees wanted him for murder, but not too bad because the one he shot that day was not too valuable either."

"Why ain't the marshals got him?" Hamp asked. Hearing his wife calling, he started to get up. "Coming," he called back.

"They have tried, but he knows the country too well and people hide him because he bribes them with whiskey or scares them to death."

"Horsekiller, stay and have breakfast with us."

"I will."

Hamp stretched his arms over his head. "Better go see what she wants."

Horsekiller nodded he understood. "Same reason why I better go home." Then in the half light a big knowing grin spread over his broad dark face.

Chapter 18

In the morning Hamp paid Mary for her care of his partner. Rebecca and her mother, Wanna, asked to go along and he thought it a good idea if they were willing to tend to his partner, so he agreed. Clint never said yea or nay, but he needed a nurse and everyone else was busy. So with Wanna, a large older Indian woman he had to boost on the butt to get her in, and Rebecca in the back of the wagon with the patient, they started for the herd.

Hamp took his time. The road was rough enough with an iron-rimmed wagon, never mind the pallet they had in the back for Clint. Every bad bump probably hurt Hamp more than it did his wounded passenger. They stopped at a creek ford for lunch and Hamp hung feed bags on the team. The women served light bread and cold meat left over from breakfast.

"You cowboys eat plenty good," Wanna said with her mouth full of food. Then she laughed aloud. "Bet Horsekiller misses your food."

Seated cross-legged on the ground beside the woman, Hamp asked, "Reckon that's why he stayed with me so long?"

She shook her head and her long coarse black hair waved on her full shoulders. "No, him damn good man. He say you one good guy too."

Hamp nodded that he heard her. He thought the same of the Indian. Perhaps he should scout north when they were all settled and see the condition of things for them to move closer to Fort Smith. Plus he wanted to ride in and see the broker Paulson and discuss the final deal on the sale.

This rolling Indian land was good grazing, but he yearned for the hill country of Texas. Maybe it would rain that fall and winter down there. This country they were in had had rainfall. The small creeks still flowed water this late in the summer. It would soon be fall too. With the shorter days and longer nights the day's heat was dissipating more.

They arrived at the herd in late afternoon. Drying his hands on his apron, Sam rushed over to see about Clint. Hamp nodded in approval at the older man's questioning look before he peered over the side boards.

"You old sumbitch, how are you?" Clint asked and the whole conversation forced Hamp to jerk around and frown at the patient. Then shaking his head at the concerned Junie, he decided it was all show. Clint never offered to get up. A part of the deal that niggled Hamp more was that when he and Rebecca had gotten Clint out of the wagon so he could relieve himself a few times, the shrunken form of Hamp's once stout friend was scary.

"Everything all right?" he asked Sam.

"Fine. I hadn't heard anything went wrong today."

"Good." Hamp turned to his wife. "I'll saddle a horse and circle the herd."

She agreed, then stood on her toes and kissed him. "Don't forget to come back for supper."

"I won't." He laughed at her chiding.

It felt good to be back in the saddle as he short-loped the horse for the grazing cattle. He reined up short of spooking them and saw Miguel coming from a hilltop to join him. One of the boys was driving in some wanderers.

While he waited and watched, a black steer raised his left leg so he could reach back to scratch a spot in his back with his long horn. His obvious fat condition made the effort harder and he licked his dark nose twice when he finished. The hair on his hide shone in the afternoon sunshine. Long way from the drought-starved critters they'd brought out of Mexico only a few months earlier. Hamp hoped that Clint got well enough soon to see the transformation in the herd.

"Any trouble?" he asked Miguel.

"No. I saw a rider late yesterday who looked like he was snooping around, but he disappeared in the timber and I never got a good view of him."

"This outlaw McKay is redheaded. He's short, according to Horsekiller, and I suspect crafty."

"He's the one who shot Clint?" Miguel asked.

Hamp nodded. "Horsekiller went home, but he said to watch out for him and if he heard anything to let me know."

"Where's Clint? Didn't you get him?" The youth frowned and looked around.

"I brought him back, but he's still too weak to ride a horse."

A concerned expression formed on the youth's face. "Must be bad."

"He is. How are the rest of the boys?"

"Good. Juan had a bad fall with his horse going after some strays, but he's going to be fine. Hard to kill a good Mexican." Both men laughed.

"I want to edge them north," Hamp said. "I'll ride that way in the morning and look for some more grazing."

"Good idea. Plenty here, but if we were closer I'd feel better."

Hamp agreed, looking over the rolling country and the herd. Where was McKay? Horsekiller had no reason to warn him unless he believed what he said. The hands working this herd meant a lot to him—he wanted no big shoot-out in the midst of the drive.

Back in camp, he took the cup of coffee that Sam handed him. Squatted down on his heels, he blew on the hot brew.

"Cattle all right?" Junie asked, joining them.

"Doing the best. I'm going to ride ahead in the morning and check on the grass. I shouldn't be gone long. How's Clint?"

"He's still too weak to walk by himself," Junie said and shook her head.

Hamp nodded, feeling grim about his partner's condition. "Reckon he needs a real doctor to look at him?"

"I don't know," she said softly. "He's just very weak."

"I wish I knew a good doctor we could take him to. Maybe there's one in Fort Smith. Not like him to be down this long."

"Be careful," she said cheerfully. "Rebecca has gone to pick some ripe plums. I am making some dessert with them for the crew."

"I'll be back for supper."

"Good," she said and hurried off.

Hamp left camp and rode north. He kept to the hilltops, riding a long ridge, then noticed the bank of clouds gathering in the west. Might be a thunderstorm by dark, he decided, pushing the horse along.

He dropped off into a deep swale and found a live-water creek. Willows choked the bank and he was forced to use a crossing. Then up the next slope, he rested the pony on the hogback. The mix of grass didn't look as strong on this ground—more sedge and less switchgrass and taller bluestems. He'd have to drive the herd through this area.

Further north, he knew of some better places to hold them over. He rode wide of some small farms, making mental notes to avoid them with the drive. Longhorns had little respect for small pole and rail fences protecting gardens and crops. No need to anger the residents or destroy their only source of food.

Junie's words about not missing supper forced him to rein up. They'd have to make a couple of day's drive to reach a place where he felt certain there was better grazing. He turned the pony back and short-loped him. In the creek bottom he spooked up some wild turkeys that flapped away in an explosion of wings.

The thunder growled in the west in the cloud formation shielding sundown. He wondered if he'd make camp before it struck. He hoped Miguel had the cattle in a herd or they could lose some.

In sight of Sam's wagon top on the hilltop, the first rain struck him. Wind threatened the fly on the wagon, and the shelter Rebecca had made to shade Clint looked endangered flapping in the strong force. Hamp shook out his slicker and booted the horse down to his wife outside looking for him.

"I better go help the boys," he told his anxious wife.

She nodded that she'd heard him over the crackling outburst of wind, rain, and thunder. Green oak leaves blasted by them on the next gust. He forced a smile to convince her it was going to be all right.

"Get under the fly," he said as he left.

The horse refused to head into the storm, but Hamp's spurs sent him onward. The day had turned to night and the driving surge of the rain changed the hot air to ice. Soon hail began to pelt his slicker and he pulled the brim of his hat down. He could hear the upset cattle bawling and in flashes of lightning saw the milling steers. He undid the lariat to wave and try to keep them in one group.

A blinding bolt struck a nearby tree and the air was full of a sulfurous stench. Flames outlined the fresh scar cut in the tree's bark to where the roots smoked at the base. He gulped a deep breath. Another fifty feet and he'd have been in that very spot.

He shouted at the top of his lungs to turn back the steers looking in his direction for a place to run. "Damn you, stay hitched!"

But his words fell on deaf ears. Three went to his right and before he could spin the horse around a dozen more fled past on the left. He could hear the other hands shouting over the storm, but the incisive bawling grew louder— nothing could hold them. They tore off in all directions, unlike a stampede on the open prairie where they all ran one way like a river's torrent. In minutes, he knew his fortune was fast racing away. Even his attempts to stop them with his horse failed. They darted past him and, filled with fear, sought some haven from the hell going on around them.

Hamp closed his eyes. They'd be lucky to get half of them back. Maybe they wouldn't run too far.

"Juan's brother Pablo is under his horse!" Miguel shouted and waved for him to follow.

They bailed off the southern slope and saw that the downed horse had become tangled in a fallen post oak. Pablo's leg was under the struggling horse that two of the others were trying to get off the moaning cowboy.

Hamp jumped off his mount and raced over. He caught the flailing animal by the head. They literally hauled the cow pony to its feet and off Pablo. Once relieved of the weight, the young man went to squeezing his leg.

"Broken?" Hamp asked.

In the slashing rain, Pablo shook his head. He didn't know, but for sure it hurt him, was what Hamp got from his reaction.

"We'll load you on a horse. May hurt, but we have to get you to camp."

Pablo nodded. "The cattle—we couldn't hold them."

"We'll get them back," Hamp shouted over

the storm. He knew good and well they would—even shorthanded. Thunder rolled over his head and rain made a gusset out of his hat and ran in a river in front of his face. Somehow they'd gather them.

Chapter 19

The stars came out in two hours. Pablo appeared to only have bruised his leg. But the swelling set in from his foot to his crotch and Junie found him some whiskey for the pain. They had him in the same shelter with Clint.

"Bad stampede?" Clint asked in his unfamiliar husky voice.

"Bad enough. The timber may have slowed them. We won't know a damn thing till daylight."

"Sorry—I ain't worth nothing."

"Get well," Hamp said. "Everyone else try to get some sleep. We'll go look for them come morning."

"Can I go?" Petey asked.

"Who'll watch the horses?"

"I can handle them," Sam said. "If'n Junie can handle the cooking."

"I can do that," she said, looking back at him from loading his plate at the cooking fire.

"I guess you can go, then," Hamp said and took the loaded tin dish from his wife. "Thanks."

He squatted in his boots to eat his breakfast. At some time, Rebecca had dug a berm around the shelter and this was probably the only dry spot in camp where the rain's efforts had not run over it.

"Will you be able to find all of them?" Junie asked.

Hamp nodded. He would have to.

His crew was in the saddle. He divided them up and they set out in four directions. He took Petey with him. In a half hour, they found a good-size bunch bedded down, chewing their cud and looking full. Hamp sent the boy to the far side and they began getting them up and moving back toward camp. Grateful that the steers were fat, he swung his rope and moved them in a bunch of about seventy-five, he estimated.

A bawl in the brush and he swung the horse around and saw three more lost-acting critters coming out of the patch of post oak. They liked to belong, a fact that made him smile. He could only hope the others had equal luck. Midday they drove their bunch in with the rest of the herd.

On horseback, Miguel came to meet them. "No sign of Juan. He went east."

"I'll ride that way and check on him. Petey, you stay here and help hold them."

"How many you bring in?" Miguel asked

"Last count I think about eighty-five."

"Good. We can't be missing many over a hundred, then."

"That's good news."

Miguel nodded.

Hamp jogged the big bay down off the hillside and rode up the grassy creek bottom hemmed in by the hills. Plenty of tracks and manure. A good share of them had headed east and would not be hard to follow. He'd probably meet up with the oldest of the Castro brothers, Juan, coming back with his portion.

But he rode on for two hours without sight of him. He cat-hopped the bay up a ridge to get a better view of the lay of the land. Then he heard cattle bawling and figured they were north of him. He bailed the bay off the ridge and soon found fresh horse tracks. Several unshod pony tracks. They might answer why Juan had not come in. Juan's horse's shod tracks were in the middle of them.

Had McKay struck his lone rider? From the sounds he could hear, those cattle were being moved and not back but rather away from the herd. He felt for the Colt on his hip as the midday heat sent beads of perspiration down his face. Once again he had left the long gun in camp, something he vowed to himself not to ever do again on this drive.

He cut west to see if he could head them off and possibly get sight of the situation. No sense riding directly in on them until he had them sized up.

A half hour later, he had hitched the bay and hiked to the rise he felt was over where the cattle thieves would pass. Belly down in the wet grass, he could see there were four riders. All wore unblocked hats and feathers. One was shouting orders at the others on how to drive the steers. He was the big fat one—probably older than the other three. Then he saw Juan Castro, bareheaded on horseback, hands bound behind his back, being led by a squaw riding a paint.

First he needed to separate his man from her, then he could worry about getting the cattle back. The direction they were headed, he would need to stop them or they'd soon be gone from his reach. But belly down in the tall grass, chewing on a stem, he wondered how he would ever manage to do it. He'd have to move further north and look for the chance to ambush them to get Juan out of harm's way.

He moved backward in the tall grass until he felt safe from their sight and then hurried to the bay. He rode hard until he came to a bushy creek crossing on the dim wagon tracks that offered enough cover for him to wait in ambush, and hoped the squaw leading Juan's horse came through the opening after the herd.

Time passed slowly. He sat upon the ground in the dense gooseberry and redbud bushes. Long before he could feel the vibration of their approaching, he could hear the cattle bawling. Horns clattered and cattle coughed on grass seeds in their throats. He heard the dull sounds of their cloven hooves on the ground and the splash as they slipped into the creek or jumped off the bank to span it. None could reach the far bank, but they sent water high in the air as the thieves shouted and cussed them.

Where was she at? He was crouched and ready. Then the older fat Indian went past and Hamp could hear the last of the cattle scramble over the rocks on the far beach. Where was she at? A yellow sweat bee buzzed around his head. He swung at it, irritated.

Then he saw her coming on the thin colt. Good, he decided and began to move. She acted half asleep and he rushed in, jerked her off the horse with a hush to the surprised Juan. He kicked her colt in the butt and headed for the brush with Juan's reins in tow. Her spooked horse jumped off the bank and ran away as she began to wail.

Hamp never looked back. In the cover of the trees he used his jackknife to cut Juan loose. He listened to the old man's cussing, but they were moving away.

"I never saw them. I had the steers headed back and they jumped me," Juan said.

"Who are they?" He listened, but they were trying to make the steers run by shouting at them.

"Red Hawk something."

"That's the old man?"

"Yeah. They're going to drive them to Fort Smith and sell them, he said."

Hamp found his spare pistol in the saddle-bags. "Here's a gun. Red Hawk better get ready. We're going to take our cattle back."

Juan shook his head as if impressed. "I was

sure surprised to see you when you jerked her off that horse. She never knew what hit her."

"Hated to have to do that, but it was the only way I could get her out of the way and not shoot her."

"Let's go get those *vacas* back," Juan said, ready to go.

"Right."

The two set out. Hamp wanted to go around the hills and head them off. One thing he knew, the steers were too fat to want to run very far, if the rustlers even got them to trot. Second, they were not experienced drovers. Anxious to intercept them, he and Juan raced down the valley, Hamp trying to visualize the lay of the land to a place where they could ambush them and head the four off.

Hamp pointed to the east and they swung up a grassy hill. Reaching the top, Hamp saw the surprised faces of the thieves. He fired his pistol in the air and the two of them charged off the hillside. The rustlers panicked. The old man took some shots at them with a black powder pistol. The range was too far but Hamp saw the smoke from the muzzle. With a hard look on his face over his defeat, Red Hawk went to whipping his horse away from the herd with the pistol.

"We got them!" Juan shouted, reining up his horse.

"Yeah, get around the herd and head them back. It'll be dark before we can get them there."

"Sí, Señor Hamp. One shot, they ran like chickens, no?"

Amused, Hamp laughed aloud at the notion. "Yes, like chickens they ran away."

Chapter 20

Midmorning they drove the steers within sight of the herd. With no sleep overnight except a nap or two in his saddle, Hamp shook his head to try and be aware at the sight of Miguel and the others coming to look for them.

"How many head did you bring back?" Miguel asked as everyone crowded around on horseback asking questions of him and Juan about their absence.

"A hundred and five," Hamp said as Juan explained about the loss of his hat and events of his capture to the other hands.

"Good," Miguel said. "We only lost seven, then."

"Best news yet. Thanks to all of you." Hamp looked over the beaming drovers and the spread-out grazing animals that had looked up at the new arrivals. A few returnees tested the

system of social order. Some head butting occurred, but soon they were resolved. Filled with
weariness, Hamp waved for Juan to ride with
him toward the wagons.

"Let's go eat."

Juan spurred his tired horse to catch up. "I'll
sure be glad to be back home."

Hamp nodded that he heard him as he saw
his wife waving at him from camp. "Yes, it will
be good to be back home in Texas. We still have
two months before we can go back. You will stay
with us."

"Oh, sí, I would never quit you and Señor
Clint. But I have this girlfriend I miss so much."
A broad smile on his coffee face, he nodded as
Junie came shouting.

"I guess I know what you mean," Hamp said,
dismounting and hugging her. Her presence felt
like a usual part of him, though he could recall
returning many times in the past and not having
anyone to hold and kiss or someone concerned
about his well-being. The whole process
warmed him inside with pride.

"How's Clint?" he asked, hoping for some
good news.

"Not much change."

Hamp looked away at the green hills in the

distance and wondered what he should do about his partner.

"Why so glum?" Junie asked, walking beside him to camp.

"Perhaps we need to take Clint to a doctor, like in Fort Smith."

"Give me your horse," Juan said and took his reins.

"About time you got back here," Sam said, bent over his low fire, sizzling bacon in a skillet.

Hamp excused himself from the two and walked to the fly.

"Good morning," he said to Rebecca. "How is he?"

She shook her head with a concerned look on her face. "He is still weak."

The old woman seated on a crate said something in a guttural language.

Rebecca shook her head. "She speaks of a witch doctor."

"If he'd help I'd sure go get him."

"That you, Hamp?" Clint asked in a raspy voice that kicked Hamp in the guts.

"Yeah. We've got the cattle back."

"I'm sure putting lots on you this trip, pard."

Hamp squatted beside his pallet. "Don't worry about me. You just get well."

Clint shook his head on the pillow. "I couldn't

get my toe in the stirrup. You know what I mean?"

"You will. You will. Keep fighting, hoss."

"Yeah." Clint closed his eyes and dozed off.

Warily, Hamp rose and nodded at the concerned Rebecca. "He's still fighting."

"Yes."

He strode back to the campfire and took a place on the ground beside Juan, who was gobbling down his plate of food, busy telling Junie and Sam the story again about him jerking the squaw off her horse and whisking him away.

"He was like a ghost," the cowboy said and took another forkful of fried potatoes and bacon.

"Ghost, you better eat too," Junie said, handing him a tin plate full. Quickly she made herself a place beside him.

"Do we need to move?" she asked.

"I think we can rent some good feed up on the Canadian and not bother people. Then we could take Clint to a real doctor."

"How far?"

"Maybe four or five days. The first day's drive the grass is not good. But the closer we get to the river the better it gets."

"But we're early."

"I know, but our buyer may have a market for

some of them. We can keep them easier on those flats than in these hills. Plus we'll be closer to the law and should have less trouble with rustlers."

"And a doctor for Clint?"

"Yeah, but we better call Clint something else. The Van Buren law might get word and arrest him."

"And I could go see my family for a visit, too?"

He nodded his agreement between bites.

So the plans to move north were made and the other hands were told the future move when they came in shifts for the noon meal. Pablo was back in the saddle, but he walked with a stiff right leg.

"How are you doing?" Hamp asked him.

"Oh, better."

"Don't walk on it too much."

"I won't," Pablo said, taking his place on the wagon tongue. Junie had gone to get his plate of food.

Hamp busied himself with the food, feeling the weariness of the long night in the saddle.

"Morning, we move on north," he said to the riders when they came in for lunch. "Two or three days we'll be at the Canadian bottoms. We should be able to hold them there until we get them sold."

He napped a few hours under the wagon's shade. Then the heat woke him and he went out to relieve one of the hands on guard. They'd all been up with little sleep, and some rest in midday might help them recover. Besides, the cattle were calm in the heat of the afternoon, many lying down, most chewing their cuds.

Hamp sat his horse under the shade of a large oak. Miguel joined him

"You had any sleep?" Hamp asked.

"Some."

"Why not take a few winks?"

"I will send Pablo to the camp. His leg—"

"You go too. Me and the others can keep them."

"Sí, *patrón*." Miguel booted his horse off to find the crippled cowboy and obey Hamp's orders.

Hamp listened to the birds in the branches above him and wondered what lay ahead. The question of what McKay might try to do was still not settled. Clint's being wanted by the law niggled him too. He'd be grateful when this drive was over and they were back in the Texas hill country.

*　　*　　*

With Miguel and Juan as swing riders, the others began to funnel the herd toward them. In the growing morning light, the cattle soon settled into a stream of three or four and formed a snakelike line. Horns clacked and individual cattle bawled, upset by the loss of some companion. Some went in haste. The stragglers rose, stretched as if bored by the whole thing and looked to be planning a day at the rear of the herd lagging along.

Sam, Petey and the women were loading up. Hamp had helped them place Clint on a pallet in Junie's wagon before he rejoined the herd activity.

He rode Casey, a big sorrel horse, and drove in a few head that he discovered concealed in the brush. But most of the animals fell in as if in fear of being left behind. The seven hundred head bawling and tramping their cloven hooves on the ground made the familiar sound of a herd on the move. A strong odor of the individual animals stung Hamp's nose. It would be a hot, humid day to move north, but he felt better just being on the way.

He swung his lariat and drove in the slackers. José Peppe, the youngest of the drovers, helped him bring in the last ones until Hamp decided they had all of them. They rode from side to side driving the slow ones and far ahead Hamp could see the herd snaking northward around a hillside. He settled in for a long day on the big sorrel horse.

At midday, they reached the rocky hills covered in sedge grass and, like he suspected, the cattle were uninterested in the coarse forage. He caught up with Miguel and they both agreed to let them rest and then push on. They were at least another day's drive from the better grazing. But the steers were still full of the past day's pasture so they wouldn't lose any weight. Still, he wanted them on the better feed as quick as he could get them there. He had put so much into getting them in good condition, he hated the thought of losing a single pound.

He'd been on cattle drives since his first one, shortly after the war. Colonel Smothers had one thing in mind—driving that mixed herd north to the Kansas market, selling it and getting back home for another drive. Hamp recalled how the herd consisted of cull cows, yearling calves, and bulls that caused trouble all the way to railhead. They gave newborn calves to settlers and Indians so they weren't held back by them. Smothers wanted nothing to keep them from moving on.

Hamp recalled the long days spent when they arrived, cutting out the various classes of cattle.

The cull cows were so worthless, Smothers eventually had them slaughtered by the crew and sold their hides for a dollar. Hamp considered the slaughtering hardly worth the sweat and stink it cost the men. The bony carcasses were left out there on the prairie to rot and feed the buzzards and coyotes. The yearlings were sold for little more than the few dollars Smothers paid for them in Texas. Out of the thousand head in the herd, the colonel sold three hundred head of steers for sixty dollars apiece.

"The damn market had dropped before we got here," the gray-bearded man in his dust-floured white suit explained as he paid them off. "But I'm going home, get another herd and come right back up here. Who wants to ride for me?"

Hamp shook his head. Clint did the same.

"What's the matter with you two?"

"I guess I'm tired of no sleep and this treeless country. Don't appeal," Hamp said.

"I'll pay a bonus if we get top price out of the next herd."

Hamp recalled that same promise in San Antonio only three months before.

"What'cha thinking?" Clint asked as they walked away from the colonel.

"I'm thinking you can't simply drive every damn head of stock you can get your hands on up here. Only thing made any money for the colonel was them three-year-old steers."

"Right. I damn sure wouldn't drive a shelly cow up here to get a dollar out of her hide and me have to skin her," Clint said as they went back to their horses and bedrolls for the long ride home.

"Well, we learned one thing. Kansas ain't no dumping ground. They want cattle they can fatten or that are fat enough to butcher."

Clint nodded, then, looked back to be sure they were alone. "Them weaned calves we brought up here weren't worth any more than they were in Texas."

Hamp agreed. The long trip with Colonel Smothers had been a lesson. Through the next years they tried different markets, each time learning more about marketing from the results and what kinds of cattle would make the most money. Their business moved from driving herds up the trail for others to their own operation finally, their home ranches in the hill country expanding each year with profits from their cattle drives.

The thing that niggled Hamp the most was Clint's condition. Why wasn't he recovering? Damn, his partner was tougher than sun-cured rawhide. He must have been even weaker than he thought when they took him to Mary's and she took out that slug.

Eaten up over Clint's dilemma, he rode into camp and strode over to the canvas shelter Rebecca had strung up for shade. He ducked underneath and saw Clint was sleeping. He nodded to the old woman they called Wanna, who sat on the ground and sewed up a torn shirt. She nodded her head, acknowledging him but offering nothing about Clint.

With a quiet sigh, he backed out. Was the day-long ride too much for Clint? He missed his partner's scouting and help. Rebecca came carrying two wooden pails of water.

"No change?" he asked her.

"No, but he did laugh."

"I guess that's something good." He nodded in approval.

Junie came over to join him and swung on his arm. "We're a day closer. And Clint laughed today."

"What did he laugh about?" he said, kissing his wife's damp forehead.

"I'm not sure about what, but he did laugh," Rebecca said.

Hamp nodded. He guessed laughing was a good sign, but the thin pale-faced person asleep on that pallet was a poor excuse for his partner.

Chapter 21

Ten days later, with the herd in the Canadian River bottoms, Hamp knew what he must do next. He dreaded the long ride to Fort Smith. Still, he needed to speak to their buyer, Erick Paulson, about the scheduled sale of the cattle as well as the market and delivery.

For the first time, Clint sat up and fed himself breakfast. He rubbed his whiskers and shook his head. "Never had anything set me this far back."

"Don't get in no rush to get up. You've been pretty far down," Hamp said.

"I hear you. I couldn't wrestle with a flea and win."

"You better listen to Wanna and Rebecca, They've been worrying about you twenty-four hours a day."

"Yeah." Clint combed his greasy, unkempt

hair back with his fingers. "Maybe I'll get cleaned up before you get back from up there."

Hamp nodded. "I'll try not to be gone over three days. Ride up there and right back."

"They can handle it. If not, then all these women around here will sure as hell chew them out." Clint laughed halfheartedly and Hamp joined in.

After his visit, Hamp rode Strawberry, the red roan, out to check on the herd and visited with Miguel.

"They like this grass better." A smile on his brown face, the youth wiped his sweaty forehead on his sleeve. "Plenty hot up here."

"Humid," Hamp said.

"Must be the river."

"Kind of steamy. I'm going to ride for Fort Smith in the morning. Keep your eyes open and have everyone carry a pistol or rifle. McKay and his bunch may try to attack us."

Miguel nodded. "We will be careful."

"Clint sat up and ate breakfast today."

"Bueno!" Miguel's face lighted up and he nodded in approval. "Be good to have Clint back."

"It'll be a while before he can straddle a hoss, but I did feel better seeing him sitting up."

"Don't you worry none. Things will be all right here while you are gone."

"Good."

The next morning before daybreak, Petey caught Cyrus, a big sorrel that could single-foot and cover lots of ground. Hamp kissed Junie good-bye and nodded to the rest. He crossed the muddy red Canadian on the small ferry and was on the Fort Smith Trail headed northeast even before the sun came over the soft blue Ouachita Mountains over in Arkansas.

Midday, he stopped at a small crossroads store and bought a bowl of stew from the large Indian woman in charge. It was tasty and he thanked her when he paid the twenty cents she asked him for. He walked outside and looked around the place. From the corner of his eye he caught a glimpse of someone on horseback in the brush watching him.

When he stepped off the porch on the dirt, the rider turned and drove his horse into the woods. The hatless rider looked swarthy and unfamiliar, but the notion of someone spying on him knifed him deep in his gut. Hamp made a mental note about the rider's long black hair and the nondescript bay horse. When he swung into the saddle he remembered something different about the animal. The pony had one ear that was half cut off.

Would they use his absence to attack the herd or try to ambush him further up the trail? He sat in the saddle with a last look at the spot where the spy had disappeared. He sent Cyrus in a long single-foot gait down the dusty wagon tracks.

Evening, he reached a small settlement, still short of his goal. He planned to grain Cyrus and take a small break, then push on to Fort Smith in the darkness. He hitched him at a rack and stepped up on the wooden boardwalk. The store was lighted by two coal-oil lamps that cast shadows.

"Hello," someone offered.

Three startled men at a side table scraped their chairs on the floor getting up, which caught his attention. Hamp's hand went for his gun butt out of instinct. His fist filled with the redwood handle and he thundered the hammer back and faced off the threesome.

"I came in here in peace. You all drop your hardware slow like. What do I mean to you?" Colt leveled at them, he tried to search their brown faces for the answer to their response at his appearance.

"You the law?" one asked.

"Hell, no, I ain't the law," he said, half cocking the revolver and clicking the cylinder around so the hammer would fall on the empty chamber. The feeling of high tension slowly drained from him.

The man in the white apron behind the counter mopped his face on a cloth. "You gave all of us a scare. What can I do for you?"

"I'm looking for something to eat and some grain for my horse."

"We can do that. I'll get your horse some grain first."

While the clerk went to fill a poke with corn, Hamp looked over the threesome, who were back to talking softly to each other. None of them were familiar faces, but he made a note of each one.

"Here you go, mister," the proprietor said, handing the feed over in a nose bag.

"Thanks. Could a man get a meal here?"

The man nodded. "I'll have the squaw fix you a plate. You got a herd of cattle?"

Hamp nodded.

"They fat enough to butcher? I could use a beef or two."

"I'll talk to you on my way back in a few days. We might have some that would suit you."

"Good. Your supper will be ready in a few minutes."

Hamp went out and hung the feed bag on the horse's head. He listened to the night insects beginning to sizzle and was grateful the day's hot temperature was starting to fade. He reentered the store and watched the men at the side table pour whiskey in their tin cups on the sly.

"Over here," the clerk said, indicating a smaller table with a chair where a large Indian woman in a many-layered dress waited with his plate of food.

Her cooking for certain did not equal Sam's or his wife's, but he had had worse. The bread was too baking-soda tasting, the meat and potatoes flat on his tongue. He finished his plate and decided he was rested enough to take on the last leg of his journey. After paying the man he went out and returned the feed bag. Then he tightened the girth, swung aboard and headed for the big city on the Arkansas.

Late in the night, he descended the sandy high bank for the ferry under the dim lantern lamps. A sleepy-eyed youth came out and collected thirty cents, then went to stoking the boiler up for steam. In five minutes there was enough power to make the paddle wheel fling water and they were backing away for the far side to cross the Arkansas. Most of the multistory brick buildings on Garrison Street looked dark. The old three-story former army barracks where the federal judge Isaac Parker held his court business sat off to the right, a light or two on in the windows.

A fishy odor assailed Hamp's nose as the ferry slapped the river current and the dock drew closer. The paddle wheel churned up a spray that felt good in the hot night air. He'd best stable Cyrus, get a room and look for Erick Paulson in the morning. A few hours' sleep would be welcome. He exhaled a sigh. Been a long day.

Sun pouring in and the morning's rising heat in the room woke him. Lying in a bed of sweat, he threw his legs over the side, sat up and mopped his face in his hands to try and become more alert. Be another scorcher, was all he could think about. No breath of air stirred the yellowed muslin curtains as he stripped out of his underwear and went to the washbowl and pitcher to wash off. The job felt like an act of futility but he finished, dressed and went down in the lobby.

Already the barkers were on the sidewalks extolling the virtues of the various dens of iniquity up and down Garrison Avenue, about the best food, tallest drinks and prettiest girls in their places.

He avoided them all and found Chang's Cafe, down the side street and in a basement. The bell rang over his head when he entered. A small Oriental rushed over to show him to a table. He thanked the five-foot-tall man and noticed various clients around the room behind newspapers and eating American food.

"Bring you flied eggs, bacon, biscuits?" the waiter asked.

"Yes," Hamp said. "Erick Paulson been in here today?"

"No see today. Yesterday he come in here."

Hamp nodded. "That's fine. I'll find him." He knew the cattle buyer usually ate breakfast at Chang's, but he might be out of town on business. The notion did not set well, for it would extend his stay, but nothing he could do if Paulson was gone but hang around for his return.

The waiter brought his food right after three men dressed in suits came inside the cafe and hung their wide-brimmed hats on the pegs by the door. They looked around as if inventorying the place and were soon shown to a table across the room. No doubt they were some of the deputy marshals for the federal court. Obviously that, for they all wore guns, as he could see from the bulges under their coats and they looked tough enough to handle themselves.

After his meal he went up the street and stuck his head in McFarland's Saloon. The cigar smoke was thick enough to cut with a knife and he was forced to walk halfway across the barroom to see the gamblers at the back table. No Paulson.

"You seen him?" Hamp asked the barkeep.

"Paulson? Not today."

He thanked the man and was grateful in ten steps to be back out in the fresher air of Garrison Avenue. He climbed to the second story of the Plate Building. There behind a desk sat the cattle buyer with his coat off.

His light-colored hair had gotten thinner and the hard first look from his blue eyes was one of a frown. "That you, Hamp? Hell, I wasn't expecting you for six more weeks. Have a seat. How's Clint?" the buyer asked after they shook hands.

"We been coming slow. Cattle are fat. Doing great. Got some good graze down in the Canadian bottoms. Clint's the biggest worry. He ain't doing much good. Got hisself shot up in a scrap." Hamp sat back in the leather chair before the desk.

"Bring him in to the doctor here and have him checked out."

"What about the Van Buren law?"

Paulson scowled at him. "Hell, they ain't got no authority over here."

"He's too weak to languish long in jail, as tough as he is." Hamp wanted some assurance about his partner's safety before he brought him into town.

"They won't bother him. I swear." Paulson raised his right hand to take an oath.

"Maybe later when I'm certain it's okay."

"Suit yourself, but he'd be safe. How many head have you got?"

"Seven hundred. All steers. Threes and fours. Should weigh seven to eight-fifty apiece."

"Sounds wonderful."

"When can we start selling them?"

"Three weeks. I've got a contract with the Creek agent for two fifty head at Muskogee. Pays ten cents a pound. I get a cent out of that."

"Sure, but how good are his scales?"

"They're nearly new. Work good."

"We need them there when?"

He pointed to the calendar on the wall. "See them red marks? That's the days in September when he hands out commodities. Steers need to be there the day before to be weighed."

"Good. We've got them sold."

"The butcher here can use ten head a week starting now. I've got five hundred sold to the Cherokees the last week in September. So I'll need to find some more. But you boys will be out of here in no time."

"What's the Cherokee contract look like?"

"Be ten cents a pound. They've learned their lesson. Adkins delivered them beef last spring. Delivered it for eight cents and the cattle looked like scarecrows. They won't buy cheap beef again."

Paulson clasped his hands over his chest and leaned back with a squeak in the chair. "Hot as hell, ain't it?"

Hamp agreed, feeling better about the sale deal. He sat back in the chair. Sweat stuck the shirt to his back.

Chapter 22

Hamp downed a cold beer in the Mule Head Bar, wiped his hand on his upper lip and walked out of the sour-smelling barroom into the morning sun. A check up and down Garrison and he saw no problems. He thought about the Indian who had been spying on him. No sign of him in the hustle and bustle traffic of the busy city street.

He spoke softly to Cyrus when he undid the reins, then checked the cinch, stepped in the saddle and nodded his good-byes to the metropolis. Headed for the ferry, he rode around the many delivery drays and wagons, some unloading, others he had to avoid for being crossways in the street for no reason that Hamp could figure.

Then he noticed a rider draw up on the other side of the street, separated from him by both ribbons of traffic movement. It was the short-eared bay that the man rode that caught his attention. He tried to get a better look at the rider with long braids and a dark hat, but the rider ripped the horse around when he saw that Hamp had recognized him and went up a side alley at a gallop, shouting for people to clear the way.

Frustrated, Hamp held Cyrus up close, looking over the confusion and the busy crowd. It was the second time that same person had escaped him—getting to be a habit that needled him.

At the ferry he dismounted and led Cyrus aboard. Whoever that spy was, he needed to know his business and who he worked for. Standing in the too bright sun on the deck he listened to the water slap the barge. He moved aside to allow a white man with a freight wagon drive his double team of big horses on the ferry. The barge shifted under the weight of the horses and wagon.

"Whoa! Whoa!" The man locked the brake and tied off the reins. A big man, he climbed down and nodded to Hamp and the ferry operator. "We heading over?"

"In a minute," the engineer said.

"Can't be too soon for me," the teamster said

and spat a big cud of tobacco in the muddy river.

"You must not like Fort Smith?" Hamp said to make conversation.

"Like it? Why, hell no, I hate it. Biggest bunch of cheats and swindlers in the world live here."

"Aw, you lost your ass again playing cards with them sharks." The engineer laughed and began stoking up his furnace with chunks of wood.

"That's all right, Kelly. I'll have me a laugh too one day, when I skin them crooked bastards within an inch of their lives."

Hamp smiled and nodded—*or when he caught them with a card up their shirt sleeve.* Poor man was no better about gambling than his partner, Clint. All those gamblers played tricks. They had to do so to survive. Otherwise, in a fair deal, the cards would turn on them and they'd be broke. He was relieved when the ferry began to back out and head for the Nation. Be good to be back with Junie and the crew.

On firm ground at last, he led Cyrus off the ferry and mounted, then with a salute and smile for the still grumbling freighter, Hamp headed for camp a good two days' ride away.

At nightfall he stopped at a crossroads store and had a meal with the white proprietor and his Indian wife. Then he fed Cyrus some grain and put him in a small stall with a manger full of hay. No threat of rain, he laid out his sogans beyond the corral and sought a few hours shut-eye. If he rose early enough he could by his calculations be across the Canadian by late afternoon.

Almost asleep, he heard some riders rein up at the store building, and eaten up with suspicion, he grabbed his Colt and listened intently.

"Where is he?" someone demanded.

"Who?"

"The white man rode in here an hour ago."

Hamp's hand grew wet around the grips on the .44. They were looking for him. Too dark to see who they were except for the shapeless hats they wore that made an outline of their heads. The spy on the bay might be with them.

"Gawdamnit, where is he?" The voice sounded short on patience.

Filled with anger, Hamp made his way swiftly around the pen. They wanted him, they were about to find him. He stepped gingerly in his stocking feet and soon had the intruders in his gun's range.

"I'm here! Who in the hell's asking—"

The darkness flamed orange with gunshots when they turned to shoot at the voice in the night. Horses screamed in panic and some animals charged away under the barrage of bullets exchanged. Men shouted in pain, then a double-barrelled shotgun answered their protests. The others fled. Silence reigned, except for the raspy breathing of a badly hurt horse.

Hamp reloaded his handgun using the starlight to see. Walking carefully toward the store in his stocking feet, he wondered if the shoot-out was over.

"You all right?" the storekeeper named Winslow asked from the front porch.

"Yes. Who the hell were they?"

"Quin McKay and his gang." Winslow held up a light and his Indian wife carried the double-barrel Greener for him. "He ain't got as many guys as before."

With his boot toe, Winslow turned the first limp body over. Obvious that one wouldn't shoot at anyone anymore. The other raider lay on his back and blood showed at the corners of his mouth when Winslow held the lamp over him.

"What did you want me for?" Hamp asked him, after making certain the wounded raider was disarmed.

The Indian's dark eyes went blank and Winslow shook his head in disapproval. The buck was dead. "Guess he didn't know. What're you looking at?"

"This dying horse," Hamp said, staring at the cropped ear on the downed animal. "Whoever rode it in here was the same one's been spying on me the past week."

"One of them?" Winslow indicated the two dead men.

Hamp shook his head. "This one had long hair hung down the middle of his back."

"Oh, you mean Quin hisself." Winslow frowned and his woman nodded in grim agreement.

"Never met him before in my life, but I've seen him several times, stalking me. I thought McKay's hair was red."

Winslow shook his head. "He dyed it a while back so no one would know him. You're lucky to be alive."

"If you'll be all right I'll ride on," Hamp said to the man. "I'm concerned about my people and the cattle herd."

"McKay must want it," the squaw said and Hamp noticed for the first time in the lantern light the three gold coins that hung around her neck complete with blue and red beads. Different kind of decoration, he decided, and nodded in reply to her.

"Maybe he does. Thanks for everything. Hope I didn't bring you folks any trouble."

"We have to sleep with our guns. The day will come when someone will deal with McKay. Maybe some of Parker's men will handle it."

"Do they want him?"

Winslow shook his head. "I don't know, but he'll slip up and break a federal law and they'll arrest him."

"Thanks." Hamp shook the man's hand and nodded in gratitude to the woman. He walked gingerly back to his bedroll and sat down to wipe off his socks and pull on his boots. In his present state, he was too keyed up to sleep anymore anyway.

He reached the ferry at daybreak. Woke up the operator and loaded Cyrus on board for the man to winch them across. A damp, fishy smell from the river filled his nose while the old man complained about the hitch in his back with each tug on the handle.

Hamp had more things on his mind than the old man's aches and pains. How was Junie? His crew? And Clint? He paid him the twenty-five cents and rode on. After an hour at a long trot he pulled up and studied the cattle spread out grazing. Thank God they were still there.

"Got here just in time," Sam said. "Food's on."

He slipped wearily from the saddle. "Everything all right?"

Sam sort of nodded and Hamp frowned. "What ain't?"

"Well—" Sam began and then shook his head. "You ain't been here to do none of the damn work." Then he burst out laughing and slapped his knees.

Junie rushed up and hugged him. "You're back."

"Part of me anyway."

"Part? What part did you lose?"

"My butt, I think, but it'll ride in an hour or so."

She laughed and put her head on his chest to rock him in her tight embrace. "Good for you to be home. Or here, anyway."

"How's Clint?"

"Not much better."

Chapter 23

The coolness of the predawn would be the only escape from the day's heat and humidity. Dampness off the dew on the grass invaded his boots. Hamp considered the soft light in the sky that preceded the sun's rays.

Clint wasn't a whole lot better or stronger—no fever that he could tell, simply not regaining his strength. In his own internal reasoning, he thought perhaps a real doctor from Fort Smith would come across the river into the Nation and look at him when they got closer. Despite the cattle buyer's thoughts on there not being a problem for Clint to come to Fort Smith, Hamp knew his partner could not survive being jailed in his condition.

"What next?" Sam asked as he hustled around the campfire preparing breakfast for the crew.

"Guess we better move closer. Peterson thinks

the market is good. We should be able to sell all of them in the month. So we need to be closer."

"When we going to do that?"

"In the morning."

Sam nodded that he heard him. Junie came from the back of the chuck wagon with a bowl full of dough for the dutch oven.

"Think I could ride up home then?"

Hamp nodded, realizing how anxious his quiet wife was to see her kinfolks. "I can take you up there when we get the herd settled in somewhere."

"That'll be fine," she said and grinned big at Sam. "Want me to help you make them?"

"Land, girl, I'll never get them fed without your help."

"You just say that, Sam. You could feed an army and never miss me."

"I dang sure will when you're up there."

Hamp poured himself a cup of coffee using his kerchief for a potholder. Those two had lots of fun doing hard work. Another neat part about his wife, she never figured she was too good to pitch in. Maybe her sister's poor treatment of her made her that way. The way Sam bragged on her all the time, Hamp could see the blush it drew many times. Junie sure wasn't used to much praise in her life. Good for her, and she deserved it. He sipped his coffee, still concerned about Clint's lack of recovery lying up there on a pallet under her fly.

He spoke to Miguel at length about moving the herd. The plan to drive them past Yoe's store on the first day would be far enough after the morning river crossing. The river was down, but not hard-bottomed, and the steers would have to swim. Be some get sucked in the mud. He'd hate to lose any of them this close to market.

Hands came in to eat breakfast. Others stayed with the herd. Hamp noted they all carried rifles in their scabbards. They might need them if McKay tried to take the herd. No telling what that renegade would try next, but he suspected strongly the breed had his eyes on the herd.

With his plate of food, Diego smiled when he came by to speak to Hamp. "Are there any pretty girls in Fort Smith?"

"Can't recall seeing any." Hamp laughed. "Guess I wasn't looking, amigo."

"I went to Kansas once and all the girls up there were ugly as pigs."

"Oh, I think Fort Smith has some pretty ones."

"Good." Diego nodded and went off to eat.

Hamp recalled his first trip to Abilene with Clint and Colonel Smothers. His own experience with a shady lady said Diego wasn't far from wrong—they weren't very good-looking and most hadn't had a bath since the past spring. Whew, it about turned him away from women. He was grateful for his Junie and the fact he didn't need to frequent those places anymore.

"You better eat," she scolded, shoving a plate of eggs, meat and biscuits into his hands and breaking his thoughts.

"Yes, ma'am."

She wrinkled her nose, then hurried off to help Sam some more. Spoiling that old galoot is what she was doing. Maybe ol' Sam needed that, with him dragging that stiff leg around.

After breakfast he went and sat on the ground in the shade of the canvas fly and talked to Clint.

"Moving them north in the morning. We can start making cuts when we get up there. He's got several markets and a local butcher needs some."

"Wish I could help." Clint sat up with his back braced against a wagon wheel.

"You just get well."

"How long's it going to take? Forever?"

"We'll get a real doctor to look at you when we get closer to Fort Smith."

"What the hell can he do?"

"Maybe tell us what to do."

"I'm losing faith, pard. Nothing ever kept me down this long."

Rebecca moved to put another pillow behind his back. "You are stronger."

"Hell, if I was stronger, a gawdamn baby could whip me."

Satisfied the pillow was a better support for him, she nodded in approval and started to rise. "You have the strength to cuss, anyway."

"You watch him. I am going to take a bath," she said to Hamp.

Hamp nodded that he would do that for the handsome woman. She went about getting a towel and a hairbrush, then left them.

"She's been taking good care of you," Hamp said when they were alone.

"If I ever get well enough I'd marry her."

"You could do worse."

"I learned a lot laying here. You come out smelling good with Junie. I always worried I'd put a ball and chain on your neck over that deal. Never did. You got a good woman. Hardworking."

"I won't complain. Tell me about the robbery and McKay."

"I'd been by to see 'Becca and found a card game on my way back and won some money in it. I'd had a few drinks in this place and I was going to ride back that night to the herd." Clint shook his head and combed his fingers through thinning hair.

"Guess they were watching me the whole time and a few miles down the road they jumped me in the dark. I think I got some of them, but one of them got lucky and shot me. I managed to hide off in the brush, then made my way back to her place somehow, McKay and his bunch looking for me the whole time. I saw and heard them but I managed to shake them."

"He came looking for me too. I've got a notion he wants to try to take the herd."

"Miguel said you told the boys to all pack rifles."

"Precaution. We move in the morning and get closer to Fort Smith, still he might try something."

"I wish I could help."

"Get stronger. You be all right? I need to talk to Petey about the horses."

"I damn sure ain't going nowhere. I'll be fine. You be careful. There's just one of us now."

Hamp nodded and rose. "I will, hoss."

He found Petey eating his morning meal and squatted beside him. "We'll cut out horses in the morning before breakfast. Need the good swimmers. You can take the horses across and the boys can help, then we'll bring the cattle."

"Float the wagons?"

"No." Hamp shook his head. "They can use the ferry. Save us half a day's work."

"Good. I'll think about the swimmers today that we'll need. That baldface horse of Pedro's is good in the water."

"There's some better than others. You know them."

"I'll pick 'em. We going to sell the herd soon?"

"After we get up there and over the next couple weeks we'll sell them. Why, you anxious to get back home?"

"Yeah, sort of." The boy grinned big.

"So am I, Petey, so am I." He clapped him on the shoulder as he got up.

Later that morning Hamp rode through to admire the scattered cattle as they grazed. Some lifted their heads with mouths full of grass to learn his intentions, then as if satisfied went back to cropping more forage. He drew up on the ridge where Miguel sat his dun.

"They're fat for longhorns," the youth said.

"They look good. Been a lot of work for everyone, but I think we've done well."

"You think McKay will still try and steal them?"

Hamp nodded. "There isn't much wealth to steal in the Nation. No stage lines carrying more than mail, and the railroads are well guarded."

"But how would he sell the cattle?"

"Damned if I know, but I still think they're a tempting apple."

"What did he and Clint have a gunfight over?"

"What I get from Clint, he and his gang tried to rob him."

"Why does McKay want to kill you?"

"I guess thinking then he could steal the herd easier. McKay don't think like a rational person to my notion."

Miguel nodded. "I tell the boys to be ready for trouble all the time."

"That's the best we can do."

Miguel took off his sombrero and wiped his face on his sleeve. "Sure is humid up here."

Hamp smiled and agreed. "Keep an eye out."

"I will."

Back in camp, Hamp found his wife busy making pie with dried apples and raisins. Her hands white with flour, she was rolling out the dough.

"I'm making them a treat before they have to go to working so hard," she said.

"You'd spoil an old grouch," he said and

looked up to see Clint using a crutch coming from the fly. A concerned Rebecca was close by to steady him in case he started to fall.

"Got to get my strength back—" Clint was obviously out of breath from the short walk.

Hamp set him up a canvas chair to sit on. Clint nodded and accepted it, leaning on the crutch.

"Still weak as a baby," he finally managed to say.

"You'll get stronger."

"When?"

"Clint, if I knew that I'd be doctoring 'stead of herding longhorns to Fort Smith."

Junie and Rebecca laughed at his words.

"Maybe a piece of my pie will help you," Junie said.

"I'd eat two if it would."

Later that night in their blankets, Junie whispered to him, "Clint's not better."

"Takes more time than we think, I guess."

She snuggled her subtle form against him and began to arouse him. "You be careful. I've missed having you to hold me every night you've been gone."

Hamp nodded that he heard her and kissed her sweet-smelling hair. In the morning they'd move north.

Chapter 24

Steers up and bawling. They sensed the cowboys' purpose like they had been telegraphed individually the news—*we're moving today*. Hands rode up the draws to gather in the strays. Stiff post oak tore at the riders' bullhide chaps as they busted through the thickets to bring in the individuals.

Horns rattled hitting each other when crowded up by the rider toward the main bunch. Single steers that got separated from their usual group bawled like calves lost from their mammy. Familiar sounds that Hamp recalled from the many drives he'd made. On Billy Boy, a big stout sorrel, he rode after a black steer headed back for Texas rather than Fort Smith. Riding the sorrel hard, he skirted the bunches of brush and soon was ahead of the errant one and had him turned and headed back down the flat for the others. Beating his lariat coils on his chaps to make a popping sound hastened the black one's return. His loud "Hey! Hey!" was added noise to correct the animal's ways and get him where he belonged.

Point riders in place, the herd funneled north like a well-oiled machine. Once on the way, the steers soon recalled the routine and got back in the beat. Both wagons were headed for the ferry and would meet them at camp that afternoon. Petey had the horses across the river. The herd came next.

The bank offered a good level entry to the water and slightly downstream was an excellent exit point. The river's level was low, which Hamp appreciated.

Miguel's big red lead steer that he called Royal had taken the herd through the others like a pro, so Hamp felt certain the crossing should go smooth. The horses barely had to swim to get over it earlier. But he also knew that more trail hands drowned than were ever killed by guns on the drives. River fords were lined with crude crosses for the ones lost. Some of the worst ones looked like Civil War battle sites.

It being fall made a big difference. Springtime, the flow would have been up ten feet and trees plus debris coming down would have posed lots more obstacles. He knew the leaders must be about to start in and so he rode to a high place to watch for any trouble. Under him, Billy Boy stomped his hind foot at a biting heel fly.

One more river to cross—some kind of theme to this cattle driving. The line of dark-colored bovines slicing the reddish water settled him. Maybe this one would go smooth too. He needed smooth things to happen. This trip had been a worrisome one from start to finish. Muldoone's deal back in Texas wasn't settled either. He booted the horse off the hillside—better finish the crossing.

By late afternoon the herd was past Yoe's store. Hamp stopped off and paid the man for the supplies that Sam had picked up earlier.

"Watch yourself," John Yoe said, bent over the counter making him a receipt. "Word's out McKay wants you dead."

"He better have his funeral expenses cleared."

"He's tough." A reflection of light flashed off Yoe's glasses when he looked up. "Be careful."

"I'm keeping an eye peeled."

"I heard about that shoot-out you had with him at Winslow's. The light-horse police want McKay now too." Yoe handed him the receipt.

"Maybe they'll get him. Who is that Indian has the grassy creek bottoms north of here?"

"White Feather?"

"That's his name. I'm going to lease some grass from him to hold the herd while we sell them."

Yoe agreed but his lips were tightly pursed. "You watch for McKay."

"Thanks." Hamp left the store and headed for camp. Come morning, he planned to go see White Feather.

Cattle were spread out grazing and lying down when he reached the herd. Something had made him feel antsy the entire ride back. He had used some tricks to try and fool anyone following him by doubling back but found nothing on his back trail. So by the time he headed off the hillside for the creek bottoms and the wagons he began to scold himself for being so overwrought about being followed.

Lots to do when you lost your right arm's help Clint did many of those things like ride ahead and make arrangements. Hamp's job usually was tend to the herd and the drovers.

Junie met him and held the reins as he stripped the saddle off the tired horse.

"Have a good day?" he asked.

She wrinkled her nose. "No problems. It's better now you're here."

"Lordy, girl, you ain't got much to look forward to, then."

"Hamp Moser! I do too."

He dropped the saddle and hugged her. "Hey, I was only kidding. Don't stop being ready to welcome me. I feel like a king coming back to you."

She drew her face back, shook loose the hair from her face and smiled. "Then I'm your queen?"

"Yeah, sure are." He looked toward Rebecca's fly. "He any better?"

"I don't think so. He ain't walked none on that crutch today."

"Thanks. I better go see how Sam's doing."

"Doing fine. Cooking a big ham he got at Yoe's."

"How's that new dress coming?"

"Oh—" She looked away. "I'll get some time later to finish it."

"Why's that?" he asked as they headed for the chuck wagon.

"I might not fit in it for long," she said.

He looked down and frowned at her. "Fit for long?"

She looked up. "We're going to have—a baby."

Hamp simply nodded his head. My gosh! He'd almost given up on the notion.

"That's wonderful news!" He hugged her shoulder and kissed her forehead as they went along.

"You know all babies don't make it into this world."

"You concerned about the baby being all right?"

"Some."

"Aw, don't worry. Our baby will be fine."

"You always make me feel good—even when I worry."

"Supposed to—why we got married."

"You're right."

"Sam, you get enough supplies?"

"Enough for a while. This bunch eats like starved wolves and grizzly bears." The cook stood up from stirring his beans and scowled through his whiskers.

"Yeah, but they work hard."

"Part of the time."

"I'll go check on Clint," he said and excused himself. She and Sam went to talking about the night's dessert.

Hamp stopped at the edge of Rebecca's canvas shade. "How's he doing?" he asked the Indian woman.

"Weak today. Slept all day, couldn't stay awake, he said." She bent over and pulled the blanket up to cover him better.

"Fever?"

She shook her head. "Something is stealing his strength."

"I hope a doctor can help him when we get closer to Fort Smith." He nodded to her, ready to leave. "Need anything?"

"No. Only for him to get well."

Hamp agreed and headed back for the cooking area. Miguel was coming in. He needed to talk to him. The picture of Clint's flushed face on the pillow had not encouraged him any. Damn, he had enough things going to keep an army busy. And his wife was pregnant. That would be nice.

At dawn, he took Thunder from the remuda, jammed a Winchester under the scabbard, and after breakfast kissed his wife good-bye. He instructed Sam and Miguel to move about five miles north and make camp on Crib Creek. He figured he'd be back after dark.

The wagon tracks headed north across some rolling grass country. He trotted the bay horse and was coming downhill when a rider came out of a copse of post oak to his right, carrying what looked like a six-gun in his hand. Hamp jerked out the Winchester, hearing the rider screaming at his horse or something.

How many more were there? He reined the big horse around and saw nothing but the wind-tossed seed tops of the tall bluestem and other grasses. What the hell was the matter with this madman?

A loud pop of the cap-and-ball pistol and Hamp could make out the smoke at the muzzle. The rider was coming up the wagon tracks, bearing down on him. Crazy. He couldn't think of a conceivable reason for this desperate attack—unless there were more of them lying in wait. No sign of them, though.

He dismounted and put the rifle butt to his shoulder. Through the buckhorn sights, he could see the screaming banshee coming at him.

He squeezed off the trigger and the youth, hard struck in the chest by the bullet, went flying off his horse. The pony veered to the side and Hamp stood up to search around for any more signs. Without the attacker's yelling, the wind and the crows were the only sounds.

He walked toward the fallen rider. His finger on the trigger, rifle reloaded, ready in case it was a ploy or a trick. Hamp kneeled beside the prostrate boy, whose arms were flung aside, and felt for a pulse at his throat. Nothing. Still wary of the strange episode, he went for his horse.

In a short while, he had the still body wrapped in a blanket and loaded over his own pony. He had seen this boy before—but could not place exactly where. He was perhaps sixteen. Whatever drove him on such a suicidal charge? McKay no doubt was behind this. Still didn't make good sense—but lots of things didn't do that on this drive.

He rode into White Feather's grassy bottoms in midafternoon. The big man was seated in a rocker on his porch, smoking a pipe. His new unblocked hat sat squarely on his head over the shoulder-length white hair that came to the collar of his threadbare coat.

"I knew you were coming," White Feather said and stood up with some effort and smiled at Hamp. "They say your friend is dying from a bullet?"

"Not the bullet. News travels fast. Look at this boy and tell me who he is."

"What killed him?" White Feather asked.

"A bullet," Hamp said. "He came charging me like a madman, shooting and kept coming. I had to drop him."

With a handful of the dead man's hair, White Feather raised the face up and looked hard. "His name is Boo Hoo. They have fifty-dollar reward for him at Tahlequah."

"I don't have time for that. Can you have him buried?"

"You don't want the reward?" The Indian's

brown eyes opened wide in disbelief. He motioned for Hamp to go back to the porch with him.

"You can have the reward. So he's buried. Now the grass?"

"You bring some whiskey?" White Feather indicated for him to be seated in the straight-back chair beside his rocker.

"No." Hamp shook his head.

"Clint always brings whiskey."

"Don't have any. Besides, I don't need any trouble with the law."

"They say that McKay shot Clint."

"He did, but Clint's recovering."

"Good man. How long you be here?"

"A month perhaps."

"How many cattle?"

"Oh, seven hundred."

"Thirty cents a month." The Indian crossed his arms over his suit coat like that was his best offer.

"Clint said pay you twenty cents a head."

"Him and me drive hard bargain over whiskey. You no bring whiskey."

"You can take Boo Hoo's body to Tahlequah for the reward for the rest."

White Feather nodded. "Take his head in gunnysack up there. All I need."

The idea of decapitation about made Hamp gag. No love lost over the stupid dead Indian, but the notion of taking a head in a tow sack sounded crude. "Good enough. Twenty cents and his head."

"Pay half now, half later."

"That's seventy dollars, half is."

"Plenty good grass." White Feather held out his hand and Hamp paid him seven ten-dollar gold pieces.

After inspecting the coins the old man nodded. "You want him horse?"

Hamp shook his head. "That's yours too."

White Feather shouted something in a guttural voice and a girl of perhaps sixteen appeared in the doorway. She must be one of his new wives, Hamp decided. Her husband gave her instructions and she nodded.

Hamp had had enough. He knew when she went to the woodpile for the ax what came next. No intention of being there when the girl whacked the outlaw's head off, he excused himself and shook hands with the Indian.

In the saddle, he listened to White Feather telling wife number whatever what she must do next. He heard the body drop to the ground after she cut the ropes he used to tie it over the horse. Time to get out of there. He put the spurs to Thunder and rode away as quick as he could.

Chapter 25

Long after the fiery sunset, Hamp rode in past the herd listening to a Mexican herder singing a song about a wild caballo as he circled the bedded-down cattle.

Sam greeted him at the campfire. "No trouble?"

"Except for one crazy buck who must have been full of firewater," Hamp said, relating the story as Junie came from her blankets to join him.

"Just one?" Sam asked.

"Yes, and he never stood a chance. Just came riding and shooting at me with an old pistol. I doubt he could have hit a bull in the ass with it."

"You said you gave White Feather the reward on this dead one?"

"Fifty dollars. He had to take him clear up to

Tahlequah. Besides, I docked his pasture rent a little too."

"I'm sure glad this Boo Hoo couldn't shoot," his wife said, chewing on a long stem of grass.

"So am I, Junie, so am I."

"Here, I'll fix you some supper," Sam said, sticking his stiff leg out so he could bend over and dish it out on the tin plate. "What do you figure McKay will try next?"

"They'll try to steal the herd like those varmints tried in Kansas that time."

Sam nodded. "About forgot about that." And handed her the heaping dish for him.

"I never will," Hamp said, thinking about that ordeal all over again like it had only happened the day before.

Masked men woke him up from a sound sleep that night. Four days short of Abilene and after three months of little sleep. Day and night in the saddle, any chance he had to close his eyes he took serious. Woke up with a gun muzzle in his face and some guy wearing a cotton sack over his head. Hamp stood up in his shirt, underwear and stocking feet being herded along with the grumbling Clint, who was swearing the whole time at their captor. Hamp felt certain Clint's mouth would get them both shot.

"You sonsabitches! I ever get you in my gun

sights I'll blow daylight clean through all of you like a sieve," Clint raged.

"Shut up," Hamp hissed at him. Damn, if Clint kept on he'd get both of them killed.

"These bastards ain't going to steal—"

The blow to Clint's head with the gun butt sent him to his knees and the second blow from the rustler put him face first onto the ground.

"I said shut up!" the out-of-control outlaw said to the prone Clint, who wasn't hearing.

"You drag him over by the fire," he told Hamp with a wave of his six-gun.

In the firelight Hamp could see the faces of those that hadn't been out on guard. Hands tied behind their backs, they all looked like they'd swallowed a whole lemon. He struggled, dragging his friend under his arms to where the gun toter wanted him. Damn, he'd warned Clint—

"You boys can start to walking back to Texas," the leader said. "We see you ugly pusses around here, we'll shoot you down. So don't stop till you swim the Arkansas.

"Two of you get under that one on the ground and take his stinking ass with you too."

Hamp read the shocked look on the crew's faces. They couldn't believe what was happening. Hell, Texas was hundreds of miles away and no self-respecting cowhand walked anywhere. That's why God invented horses. If it was only to cross the street to another saloon or whorehouse—you went in the saddle.

Dumbstruck, the drovers rose and looked around like lost geese. Only ones that wasn't tied up was Hamp and the out-cold Clint. So he'd have to pack him for a ways. He damn sure wasn't leaving that loudmouth to wake up amongst them—they'd kill him for sure.

"What about our boots?" Waco asked.

"You gawdamn reb. To the victor goes the spoils, you should know that by now. Get walking before I plug daylight through you."

The grumbling by the men was a low sound, but they started out headed south. Clint was coming to. Hamp jerked him up.

"Shut your damn mouth," Hamp hissed at him and struggled to get his shoulder under his armpit. At last with him slung over his back, he started after the others.

"Just remember, reb, this is Yankee territory. You come back you're dead," the tough guy in charge said.

"What we doing?" Clint asked in a stage whisper.

"Giving them the herd, our kack, boots, war bags, bedrolls and I guess the chuck wagon and mules."

"Sonofabitch. You get a good look at them?"

"Hell, no, they had on sacks, but I'd know that voice anywhere."

"Good, don't forget it. Ouch," Clint said, stepping on something sharp.

The colonel caught up with them the next morning in a copse of trees beside a creek. "Where in the hell is the herd?"

"Where in the hell've you been?" Clint demanded, bent over, holding his face in his hand. "Them bastards done stole everything we had."

"Who were they?" the colonel demanded.

"We ain't sure, but Hamp knows their voices."

"Get up behind me," the colonel said to Hamp. "I'll send a wagon back with food and bring all of you to Abilene."

"What you going to do with Hamp?" Clint asked.

"Try to find them. You boys are still on my payroll."

"I may need an advance," Clint shouted after them as Hamp hung onto the back of the saddle for dear life.

The colonel was going to make a race for Abilene. He had the sorrel running flat out across the prairie. Hamp wondered if they'd even make it there at this rate or if the poor pony's heart would burst.

They arrived after dark and the colonel found Wild Bill Hickok in the Bucket of Blood playing poker. After the colonel introduced himself and Hamp, he began explaining the problem and said, "They stole two thousand head."

That's when Bill looked up at the others. "Boys, I better fold."

The men around the table nodded in agreement. Wild Bill tossed down two aces. "Beat them and you can have my money." Then the lawman with the goatee rose and motioned the colonel and Hamp toward the front door.

Hamp could hardly tear himself away from the outcome of the game and the sizeable pot Wild Bill was simply walking away from, but he was forced to hurry after his boss and the marshal. When they reached the bat-wing doors, someone shouted, "We'll hold the money for you, Bill."

"Good," he said and swept his yellow hair back in front, resetting the expensive beaver hat on his head.

Dressed in a gaudy beaded buckskin coat, striped wool pants with two guns strapped on his narrow hips, he looked more showman than law. But he strode like an athlete through the night traffic in the street for his office on the other side.

"Pete," he said to the whiskered man behind the desk when they came inside, "they stole a big herd yesterday down on the Squaw Creek. Get that worthless sheriff out of bed and tell him to meet us down there at daybreak. We ain't letting no rustlers get started around Abilene."

"They stole my remuda, chuck wagon, too. I've sent a wagon after the rest of my men," the colonel said.

Bill squeezed his beard and shook his head. "We'll take them guns and ammo. They can fight, can't they?"

"They're barefooted and no pants, but they can damn sure fight," Hamp said.

"Them peckerwoods leave anything?" Bill asked with a frown

"They aimed to make it clear out of the country with all of it," the colonel said.

"Where can they go? Injuns are too thick for them to head west." Bill stared at the cold pot-bellied stove in the center of the room. "They'd about have to drive them north, say up on the Republican River, till the new brands could heal."

"Where's that?" the colonel asked.

"North. Pete, tell that sheriff we're heading

for the Republican." Bill broke out a Winchester
and tossed it to Hamp. Then one to the colonel,
who caught it with a sharp nod.

"Take about four boxes of cartridges. That
should shoot the hell out of them. Been battles
won with less ammo," Bill said and piled the
cartons on the desk. "You got a horse?" he asked
Hamp. "See you've got some new britches and
boots."

"I also rented him a horse from the livery,"
the colonel said.

"Thanks anyway," Hamp said to the lawman
for his concerns.

"Pete! Get going. He can bring his posse, if
we even need him by the time he gets up there."

Wild Bill Hickok was harder on horses than
his boss. They rode their mounts into the
ground crossing the rolling Kansas country. But
near dawn they came over a high crest and before them was a big herd spread across the land.

Bill reined up his lathered horse and nodded.
"Recognize anything?"

The colonel strained his eyes in the still dim
light. No telling. They were only silhouettes.

"I'll mosey up there and see if I can learn anything," Hamp said.

Bill let his breath out his long nose. "I guess
they'd recognize me, and the colonel, he ain't

dressed like a drover. Go ahead, but don't take any chances. Things go wrong you beat your butt back here."

Then Bill looked to the south as if in hopes some help might be coming. Hamp knew there was nothing back there. He turned the bay horse toward where he thought the chuck wagon might be tucked in a draw.

Hamp estimated that he was half a mile from the pair when he looked down in a side canyon and spotted the green box of the colonel's Studebaker wagon parked in some willows. He reined up the bay and started to turn him around when he heard a shout.

"Get that nosey sumbitch!"

Pistol shots cracked the air. But Hamp knew that the range was too long for them to have any effect. He set heels to the bay, wishing for the spurs that those thieves had stolen from him.

Bay wasn't running fast enough through the thick grass to suit him. He whipped him over and across with the reins again and again. Plus he prayed that Bill and the boss had heard those shots. Down the slope, he looked back and saw them coming hard over the crest on his trail. How much further could this give-out pony run? Not far. Going up the next slope proved a big effort. He heard the pop of their pistols and knew they weren't far back.

How much further? He topped the hill and then when the bay about stumbled he saw both men on their knees in the tall grass with their rifles ready to shoot.

"Get over here, Hamp. It's clay pigeon shooting time," Bill said.

Hamp smiled so big the corners of his mouth hurt as he bailed off the done-in gelding. He jerked the Winchester out and took two boxes of cartridges from the saddlebags.

"Coming," he said and ran over to join them.

Too late, the pursuers realized their mistake. The withering fire laid down by the three .44/40s sent horses and riders to the ground in a fierce wreck. The unseated tried to use their pistols, but the range was too far and the lever actions cut them off like weeds under a sickle. Only a few escaped, wildly pounding their horses in the direction they had come from to make their getaway.

"That should get them down to our size," Bill said. "Be careful, Hamp, but you get to check out the dead and suffering. Your hoss is done in. Colonel and I are going to their camp and get any of them that's left."

"'I'll send the sheriff over there," Hamp said. "When he gets here."

In the saddle, Bill stood in the stirrups, looking off to the south. "Do that. I still can't see a sign of him."

Midmorning Clint and the crew arrived in a wagon where Hamp waited. The drovers bailed off and looked over the shot-up outlaws and grinned.

"You done good, Hamp. Where in the hell are my boots?" Clint asked, looking at the rustlers' footwear and trying to find his stolen ones.

"Over here on this dead one," Waco said.

"Coming," Clint said, picking up his gun and holster from the pile Hamp had made. "Where's the colonel?"

"Him and Wild Bill went to get the rest."

"I'll be damned! Wild Bill Hickok." Clint shook his head as if taken aback by the notion, then hurried off to retrieve his boots.

The sheriff arrived four hours later with a posse of thirty men. He got to count the number of stocking feet swinging off the ground under a cottonwood tree, as well as the five fresh mounds covering the rest of the Bruce Larsen gang.

Wild Bill kind of scoffed at the posse's makeup privately with Hamp. "That bunch couldn't hit a Durham bull in the ass at ten paces."

He agreed, but was glad to have his kack back. He'd never expected to see it again and had found plenty of respect for the lawman that fame would follow for the rest of his life.

"Where's Wild Bill at now?" Sam asked at the end of Hamp's story.

"Him and a guy named Buffalo Bill are doing plays back east last I heard about him."

Sam nodded. "Damn shame. The West could use more like him."

Hamp agreed and hugged his wife. He wanted to ask how Clint was doing but didn't really want to broach the subject. He listened to the night insects sizzle and rocked her in his arms. Damn, he was lucky to have her.

Chapter 26

"You awake?" A familiar voice spoke to Hamp.

He forced his eyes open with a quickened heart rate and saw the outline of the unblocked hat and eagle feather in the starlight. Squatted beside his bedroll was Horsekiller.

"Who is it?" Junie whispered.

"Horsekiller. It's all right." He threw the covers back and sat up. "What's going on?"

"Didn't mean to scare you but I know where McKay is."

"Close by?" Hamp pulled on his right boot.

"Close enough."

"He have many men with him?" He reached for the second one, pausing for his answer.

"Three, four, maybe."

"What's the plan?"

"Meet Marshal White at the crossroads pretty soon. Him go with us and arrest McKay."

"What's he wanted for by them?"

"Shooting the postmaster at Echo."

"That'll get him the noose in Parker's court. Won't it?"

Horsekiller bobbed his head. "He needs it."

"You helping White?"

"Yeah. Posse man, pays dollar a day."

"I'll be back," he said to his wife under the covers. "Tell Sam where I've gone."

"I will. You two be careful. We've got one guy shot up, sure don't need another."

Hamp saddled a fresh horse from the picketed ones and took a rifle from the wagon. By then Sam was up and they talked softly about the plans.

"Keep things going," Hamp told him.

"We will. Good luck."

"We may need it," Hamp said and he rode out with Horsekiller.

U.S. deputy marshal William R. White was a short man with a bushy mustache. Dressed in a suit, he looked more like a businessman than someone out after outlaws. They met at the Devon store after midnight. The lawman had a powerful handshake when he came off the dark porch and greeted Hamp.

"Horsekiller says you're good, that's enough for me. I'd like to make that farmstead where they're supposed to be before dawn and take them unawares."

"Good idea," Hamp agreed and they left, heading through the silver-lighted farmland. A few dogs ran out to threaten them but the rest of the trip was uneventful.

Close to sunup they tied their horses in a brushy draw and followed the lawman toward a white farmhouse and barn. Horsekiller went to cover the barn. The back door was Hamp's and Marshal White intended to kick in the front one.

"They'll scatter like rats in a burning brush pile when they come out. If they don't give up when you tell them—shoot 'em. This is a bunch of killers and they don't deserve any mercy."

Hamp nodded in agreement, listening to a rain crow already up and cawing. He watched the lawman wading through the tall grass and heading around the house. Be light outside in a few minutes. He held the rifle ready in his hands.

"U.S. marshal! Hands in the air!"

A commotion began inside the house. A shot was fired and a half-dressed figure stuck his head out the back door figuring to get away.

"Hands up!" Hamp ordered and he could see the shocked look on the outlaw's face even in the half light. "Get down here and lay belly down."

The dumbstruck youth obeyed, when another about ran over him and charged down the steps.

"Stop or die!" Hamp shouted, the butt of the rifle in his shoulder and ready.

"I give up—" The second bandit hit the ground when another in the back doorway began firing a pistol. The orange flashes from the six-shooter's muzzle made him a quick target.

Hamp answered him with the .44/40 and he crumpled in a pile.

"White, you all right?" Hamp shouted, advancing on the house. By then he was joined by Horsekiller.

A turkey gobbled and Hamp knew that was some kind of Cherokee death call. He bound up the stairs with a "hold them" over his shoulder to Horsekiller.

"Watch yourself!" the Indian said behind him.

The wounded one, lying in the doorway, was hit hard enough he was no threat as Hamp stepped over him. In the gunsmoke-fogged kitchen, he switched to his Colt for a quicker shot if he needed it.

"White?" he asked, approaching the next doorway.

"I'm all right. He's upstairs."

Somehow Hamp knew from his speech the lawman had been hit. He moved into the front room and saw the marshal with his shoulder to the wall. What he suspected was so—he'd have to take the man's word for how serious his wound was.

"Just a scratch," White said, then lowered his voice as the turkey gobble filled the house. "Be careful. He ain't coming out alive. That's that death song they sing at the end. But he'd sure like to take us with him."

Hamp shook his head and moved to the steep staircase. "I never left nothing there. He can go himself."

"He's tricky."

With a nod to acknowledge White's concerns, Hamp put his boot on the first step. The grit on the sole sounded like dry twigs breaking. Then the vibrating turkey call came again.

Step by step, his back pressed to the wall, he went up. He could see White had his pistol aimed so if anything showed at the head of them, they were dead. Soon he reached the place where he could see the upstairs floor and the individual doorways to the bedrooms.

Now let out a squawk. But nothing happened except the sunlight began to invade the house and the wood somewhere creaked in protest. He could hear Horsekiller ordering the prisoners around in the backyard. Sounded like he was having them move the wounded one out of the back doorway.

Then gobbling like a wild tom, the enraged face burst out of the side room and the outlaw fired a lever-action rifle from his hip. The gunsmoke billowed up in a blinding cloud and Hamp's Colt returned fire in the milliseconds that followed. Then silence, except for the moccasin on McKay's right foot; it flopped back and forth in death's throes.

Coughing so deep from the bitter smoke that he thought he would vomit, Hamp looked through the haze at the outlaw on his back. There'd be no more gobbles. He turned, holstered his gun and used a hand on the wall to make his way down the stairs.

"McKay?" White asked, looking pained at him. He held his left arm with his right hand.

"He ain't taking no one with him."

"Good. I would have done it—"

"You better get that coat off and let me look at that wound."

White agreed.

"I'll go get a wagon," Horsekiller said.

"Do that. Those prisoners secure?" White asked.

"Tied up," Horsekiller said as if that was enough and went back outside.

"Good man," White said as he rolled up the bloody sleeve.

Hamp agreed, looking hard at the wound. It didn't look serious, but needed to be bandaged. Just a crease where a bullet had run over his forearm—lucky too. One more good thing, McKay wouldn't bother them again. He guessed he sort of evened things for Clint too, bringing in the gang as well.

In an hour the wagon that Horsekiller hired was loaded with prisoners and the two bodies, ready to head for Fort Smith. White waved his good arm as they started out and Horsckiller nodded, riding his horse and leading the marshal's after the rig.

The next week flew by. They started driving small bunches of cattle to the Fort Smith butcher and Hamp brought back a doctor to check on Clint. A young man in his thirties, Dr. Hamby looked too young to be one, but everyone Hamp asked said he was the best. It took some more doing to get Hamby to agree to make the ride out to White Feather's.

Most of the crew was standing around camp looking at their dusty boot toes and waiting for the physician's report. He was under the fly a long time, listening to Clint's chest with a stethoscope and checking him over.

"Doc, I'm a big boy. Tell me what's wrong," Clint said.

The man dropped to a packing case for a seat and shook his head. "Wish I had better news, Clint, but I think your heart blew up."

"When he shot me?"

"Maybe getting away you overdid it. We don't know much about the heart except it feeds your body blood like a bellows feeds air to a fire. Your pump isn't working right."

"Will it heal?"

Hamby rolled his lower lip inside and paused. "It might."

"What's the odds?"

"I can't say. The human body heals many things itself. But the heart has lots to do."

"You got any medicine that would do it?"

"To be honest, no. You may gain your strength back. I really can't say."

Clint held his hand up and they shook.

Hamp wanted to go kick a stump. Maybe there was another doctor—someplace. He looked up at the canvas roof over them and knew better. How would his partner take the news when it set in? Damn, damn. Not been a great day after all.

Chapter 27

Hamp saw the familiar store under the large hardwoods coming up the hill driving the team. The rented buckboard made traveling faster for the two of them. He heard Pa shouting, "They're here, Raenita May. They're here."

He glanced over at his wife and when he saw her wringing her hands he frowned.

"Junie, you ain't got a thing to wring them hands over. You are twice as pretty as your sister. You have more food put up at home than she has. And you've got our baby inside you. Now don't take no back steps. You don't have to be uppity, but you ain't the second sister anymore."

She nodded her head and smiled, then she hugged his arm. "Hamp Moser, you can sure make me feel way over six feet tall."

"Someone needs to," he said and clucked to the team.

Paw and Raenita May were on the front steps when he pulled up, stepped down and helped her off the seat. He saw the sparkle in her blue eyes and the easy smile. Then with her new dress hem in her hand she went over and kissed her pa on the forehead.

"Good to see you," she said and he beamed back at her

"My, my, Texas has sure agreed with you."

"Why, sister, I swear you've gained weight in the right places," Raenita May said and took her by the arm. "Tell me all about married life."

The two went up the steps arm in arm. Not big sister leading the younger one, but as equals.

"My, my, she sure did blossom down there," Paw said softly.

"She's a real woman and you better get ready. You'll be a grandpa this spring."

"Lord have mercy, why that'll bust my buttons over that."

"Mine too, Paw, mine too."

Hamp left her to visit and went back to Fort Smith to close the last details on the cattle sales. He met Paulson at the Chinese restaurant and they laid out the plans.

"The agent told me he was impressed after he saw the cattle you're delivering to the butcher. He's the first honest one they've ever sent out here. He sure bragged on the condition of them. Only trouble is, the butcher here wants some more."

"Don't rain between here and down home it might be hard to do that again."

"You guys are still going to drive more cattle up here, aren't you?"

"I guess, but Clint didn't get good news from that doctor."

"What did he say?"

"Must have busted his heart getting away from them outlaws that night."

"What'll he do?" Paulson frowned, concerned.

Hamp studied the cup of coffee before him and shook his head. "I wish I knew."

"Hey, I'll need more cattle—"

"Guess Sam and I'll still be in the business for a while longer."

"Let's think about early spring—bringing another bunch up."

Hamp sat back in the chair to sip the coffee and study on it. "I'll go to thinking on it."

"Do that. I'll sure need them."

The next day he drove up to pick up his wife.

He watched her move about as she told her sister and pa good-bye. New woman, someone in charge of herself, and it showed. He smiled, proud of her, and she rushed over and kissed him.

"You were right," she whispered. "We are equals."

He nodded in approval and promised them they would be back.

On the buckboard headed back, Junie looked whimsically at him. "Why, I wouldn't trade my place in Texas for two of them old stores. 'Sides, I like the guy runs mine."

"That goes for me too," he said and flicked the reins to make them trot.

There was always a letdown when the last steer was gone. He had a limp in a hind foot and they butchered him for the big fandango. Then they buried the meat wrapped in butcher paper in the sand over the two-foot-deep bed of coals in the trench to cook for twenty-four hours. His arm still in a sling, Marshal White drove out to join them, and so did Paulson with some lady of the night called Chastine. White Feather, his wives and many others were all there for the meal. Horsekiller brought two wives and four kids. The Mexican boys broke out fiddles and guitars so they had music.

They set Clint up by the wagon so he wouldn't miss anything and Rebecca fussed over him. Wanna conversed with Horsekiller's older wife and the younger one helped Junie.

"Going back to Texas?" White asked on his second plate of food.

"In the next few days."

"Sure appreciated your helping me. You ever need any work I'd put your name in for deputy marshal appointment."

"I ever need work I'll look you up."

"Do that," White said and took a place on the log.

"Going all right?" Junie asked, coming by with more sourdough biscuits on a plate.

"You better stop and eat. It's going fine."

"I will. You know, Hamp Moser, I wasn't all that set on leaving home that first time. But brother, I'm sure glad you happened by." Then she threw her head back and laughed aloud. "Land sakes if I'm not glad."

Chapter 28

They drove from Fort Worth home in the rain. Deep ruts in the road rocked her and Hamp back and forth on the seat all day long and the creek crossing proved boggy. The remuda looked like drowned rats and the week-long drive saturated everything to the skin.

Their last night in camp before they got to San Antonio, with rain streaming off Sam's beard he shook his sodden felt hat while pouring coffee. "First it can't rain, then it can't stop. I'd take me a day or two of dust."

"Think how good the fishing will be," Hamp said.

"Hell, I don't fish."

"You could learn how."

Petey and Miguel were going to take the horses to his place, then Miguel was going over to Clint's place and be his foreman until he recovered. Listening to his partner's deep cough didn't encourage Hamp any. But no one would get well in a swamp and he hunched his shoulders against the wind that had whistled down out of the panhandle, cold for early fall.

"Reckon my fingers will ever unwrinkle?" Junie asked from beside him. She revealed the deep furrows in them.

"In time they will," he promised her. "Why, a day shopping in San Anton and you'll be just fine."

Hamp turned his attention back to the crew. "All you boys can take a week off, go home and get what you need done. We've got plenty of work to do on both ranches. Horses to break, calves to brand and work. So you report back. Our man wants more cattle too."

The brown faces crowded around under the fly nodded and smiled big. Hamp had paid them up there. But the boys kept pretty well to camp in the Nation, no doubt planning a big spree in San Anton.

The sun still had not shown when they drove on the square around the Alamo and stabled the team. Hamp helped his wife down in the light drizzle. After telling the boy to care for his animals, he took his saddlebags and a carpetbag from the back, then they hurried for the El Dorado Hotel.

At last in the lobby they stood and enjoyed the absence of rain on them. The ultimate escape made them both sleepy-eyed—for the past week in damp blankets and the cold they'd found little real shut eye. So they went up to their room, undressed and held each other in the warmth of the bed. After the nap, Hamp's mind went back to business.

"I need to go see a banker," he said.

Dreamy-looking, Junie agreed to his plan and snuggled under the covers. "Don't be gone too long."

"I won't."

He carried close to thirty thousand dollars in his saddlebags. Some were in U.S. Government warrants, the rest in cash. Their best sale ever and he would pay off all of his and Clint's debts, plus have a large enough surplus to look for more ranchland.

Banker Tom Brent shook his hand and offered him a seat. Brent, a graying man in his forties, produced a bottle and two glasses.

"You did well this trip, I suppose?"

"Best one yet. Cattle were fat and the price was solid."

"Where's Clint? Off celebrating?" Brent acted like the man might come in any moment.

"Got shot in a holdup and they say his heart isn't working right."

"You're serious? I was only kidding. What will he do?"

"Not much for a while. Doc said he might heal but gave him no promise."

"You wouldn't believe that, would you? Clint's always been the picture of health."

"It's been a shocker. When your clerk gets it all figured out, I'm leaving the rest of the money in our account. We planned to buy some more land. But I'm not in any rush. We can give him some time."

"Oh, come in, Sloan," Brent said to his assistant, who was standing in the doorway.

"Thank you. After paying off the loan I deposited twenty-seven thousand, eight hundred twenty dollars in your account, sir." And he handed him the receipt.

"Thanks, Sloan," Hamp said, checking the figures on the paper, then nodding approval.

"Good day, sir."

"How does it feel to be rich?" Brent asked

"Don't know. I've got the same problems and same wife as I had before," Hamp said with a grin.

They both laughed and toasted the future with their drinks.

Chapter 29

Texas turned to a carpet of green. The price of cattle soared and Hamp rode to Mexico in search of some steers to drive north. Raul Martinez, the best buyer he knew, said they were buying anything down there to eat all the new grass, but he would look for some good steers for him.

Hamp learned of no others for sale and was riding the big roan Strawberry north. He crossed the Rio Grande, anxious to be back home in a few days. All morning long misty weather off the coast had piled inland. The same rain that usually evaporated before reaching that far turned out to be inexhaustible. Crossing the once-baked land, he recalled rushing steers over the same country without a blade. Now it was half knee-high in weeds and six-week grasses.

He topped a rise and felt the big roan go down with a loud grunt. Then the unmistakable sound of a high-powered rifle reached him. He kicked out of the stirrups and landed free of the crumpling horse. Some sniper had killed his horse—but where was he? The Colt out from under his slicker, he turned an ear to listen for them but all he heard was the dying grunts of Strawberry. *Sons a bitches.*

His heart pounded under his breastbone. Had he been that careless? The Muldoone woman was all he could think about as he crouched behind the animal's still body. She wanted him dead.

He was miles from anything or anyone, especially anyone friendly. He thought he had steered far enough away from the Muldoone place, but obviously he hadn't. If they were robbers they would turn up shortly. He had less than a hundred dollars on his person. The light mist washed his face and sobered him. They either weren't taking any chances or aimed to be slow and calculative.

Had their first bullet been low on purpose? Being on foot was not something to look forward to in this featureless country—except for the low light, which would give him some advantage. And he had carried the Winchester in the scabbard—an additional plus for him. Canteen, some jerky in the bags. He wasn't helpless, but they did have some advantages. They no doubt knew the country. He was too far out of Mexico to go back and his nearest hope for any help was at least forty miles north.

He holstered the Colt and settled down on his butt with his back to the dead horse. If this was a game of cat and mouse, he intended to wait until dark, then move. The night would improve his chances even if there was more than one of them.

The thick musk of the horse and the smell of creosote mixed in his nose. Perhaps they would think they had shot him and would come and check. He needed to play possum. Then, when they rode up, maybe he could get the drop on them. Lots of schemes ran through his mind, but mostly he scolded himself for coming so close to them again. No, they'd got word he was in Mexico and set the trap. Still, he could have done a thousand smarter things. No use crying over spilt milk. It was him or them.

So he didn't make that dry gulcher a target, belly down beside the dead roan. He had managed to jerk the Winchester out of the scabbard—lucky the horse laid down on his left side. To stop his gasping for air, he held his breath and listened for any sound from the shooter. Only the wind.

Nothing since the long shot that took Strawberry. A good horse. He hated to lose him. Worse yet, he was forty to sixty miles away from anything, except her place. No one had ridden off, Hamp felt satisfied, since making the single shot.

Listening to the flies buzzing around the dead horse's eyes, nose and wound and mouth, he felt his own heart continue to pound inside his chest cavity. No sign of the back shooter. Perhaps the guy thought he'd wounded him and was simply waiting for him to die or show himself.

The stiff stems of long dried grass poked him. Maybe they'd come over and check. If they waited till dark they'd find the spot empty because he aimed to move out when the curtain fell. In another three or four hours he could leave the security of the horse's still form.

The time crept by. He rationed sips from his canteen. No sounds, save a small bird or the chirp of an insect. Then he heard a horse snort in the distance. Belly down, he turned an ear to listen close. The snort had been unmistakable. In less than an hour it would be pitch-dark—he and the shooter would be equal then.

He tried to imagine his enemy as the sheriff—cunning and vindictive. There was more to this game then he would probably ever know. He felt certain none of the deputies he'd seen with him were that tough. Maybe she's hired a real gunman to do him in—there were lots of toughs.

He could curse himself for not being more careful. They were either tipped off or something to know exactly where to ambush him. The sun slipped behind the distant horizon and twilight filled the land. Time for him to move. He rose to all fours.

Stars began to prick the sky. He holstered the Colt, put the strap of the canteen on his shoulder and hefted the Winchester in his right hand. Feeling stiff from lying down for so long, he kept low when he moved. The skin on the back of his neck crawled. Yet in seconds he reached the outline of some mesquites taller than the top of his head. For a long moment he stood in the cover. Should he try to circle around and find the horse he'd heard or simply move on? It might be a trap. He decided to go northwestward in the direction he'd taken Muldoone's body.

An hour passed. He kept moving, listening to sounds in the night. He could distinguish nothing but sizzling bugs. Recalling the Mexican woman's place on the way, he wondered if there was a horse there.

This was the only residence short of the ranch he'd found in several drives across this part of the country. No one would welcome him at the ranch except the muzzle of a gun. A throaty coyote yapped, causing him to pause. He stepped out again, hoping to be to her *jacal* by the time the moon rose in an hour.

Like an Indian, he scouted her place. A burro was in the corral. The notion of riding one disappointed him—it would barely beat walking.

He went to the front door and spoke in Spanish. "Is anyone here?"

"Who is it?" a woman's throaty voice hissed back.

"An amigo."

"Go away."

"No. I must buy your burro."

"Who are you?" She came wrapped in a sheet to peer at him from the shadowy room. "Oh, I see you are the gringo who shot him."

"No, I was the one took his body to her. Never mind. Here is twenty dollars."

"But—but—"

With no time for her arguments, he headed for the pen. Burro or whatever, he needed to move on. He took the bridle from the gate, speaking softly, went in and caught him, put the bit in his mouth. He led him out to the rifle standing by the gate.

"You are the one—" She wrapped the sheet tighter around her.

"Tell them I stole it while you slept," he said and leaped on its back. The animal caved in some under his weight. He reined him around, adjusting the canteen strap on his shoulder.

"You know who's out there after you, don't you?" she asked.

"No. Who?"

"The *patrón*. It is her."

Hamp felt a large rock drop to the bottom of his stomach. She was the shooter? Why would this simple woman lie? No reason. Kathren Muldoone was out there, gunning for him for something he'd never done.

He slapped the burro's backside with the rifle butt. "Gracias." And he fled into the night. When he looked back in the starlight he could see the *jacal* and the outline of the few trees. He needed to keep moving and he made the animal trot.

Hours later he drew up short of her dark outfit. She owed him a horse and he aimed to claim one. She'd shot a good one out from under him.

He stepped off the burro and turned him loose so he would go home. If he could get one of her horses, he had no more use for the short one.

He adjusted the crotch of his pants, grateful to be off the high-backboned burro, and stole closer to the pens. He could make out the windmill against the sky and the roofs of several low outbuildings. The horses were in a trap farthest away from the house.

A dog or two barked, then quit. He reached the pole fence and slipped inside, used his belt to capture a sleeping horse. Speaking softly to reassure him, he led him to the fence where someone's kack was on the fence. Once the horse was bridled, he tossed the blanket on, then the saddle. Quiet so as not to stir the lazy dog, he made sure the stirrups were close to long enough, then he mounted and drove the rest of them to the back of the pen. There he opened the gate and hissing and waving his arms set them in a long trot northward. This time the dog woke up the rest of them at the ranch with his barking, but Hamp had their saddle horses in a wad and on the run. They'd sure have to find something to ride to chase him. Perhaps the burro, if he had not started for home.

He looked back and saw lights flickering on. From deep in his throat he gave a "Hee-haw!"

and sent the remuda to running harder toward the old North Star. They'd be scattered from hell to breakfast by the time he was through with them.

He bought a fresh horse and saddle from a trader he met on the road the next day. The older man had several horses in tow and looked hard at the bay.

"I'd give you a good amount of money for him. Saddle ain't much."

Hamp shook his head. "Ain't mine to sell."

The older man nodded like he understood. "Appreciate your honesty, mister."

Hamp gave him a head bob and rode off, leading her bay. A few miles up the road he turned the stolen horse loose and slapped him on the rump to head for home. Then he set out in the opposite direction. Another twenty-four hours and he'd be with Junie. He could hardly wait. He closed his sun-stressed eyes to the notion and made the new horse lope. Why couldn't it be now?

"They shot Strawberry?" Junie asked aghast as she poured coffee and fussed over him at the table. He had been home only a short while. His wife had explained that Clint had died in his sleep the night before and his funeral would be in the morning. They'd held off as long as they could, in case he returned in time.

"Who shot your horse?" Junie asked.

"The Mexican woman said it was his wife, Kathren."

"She's gone mad."

He felt torn up not having been there with Clint in the end. Kathren Muldoone was the furthest thing he could think about. He dropped his head and shook it warily. "She sure is vindictive about it."

"Well, I'm so glad you came back to me." Impulsively she hugged his head to her breasts and squeezed him tight. "I thank the Lord, Hamp Moser, that you're all right."

"I'll be fine, but I'm so tired right now I can't hardly hold my head up."

"It's warm today. Go out back. That hammock will be the thing. I'll wake you in plenty of time to go to the funeral."

"I can use the sleep. Maybe I can get this thing about Clint off my mind too."

"Sleep. We've got all our life to live together." She herded him out to the hammock and pulled off his boots. His feet felt so good to be free, he wiggled his toes in his socks and thanked her. In minutes he was gone into deep sleep.

His dream began to shape with a woman and

three men riding up from the creek to his ranch house. Straight-backed, the woman in the saddle wore a green dress and carried a Winchester over her lap. She held up a kidskin-gloved hand and three men whose faces he could not make out stopped behind her.

"Is Hampton Moser here?" she asked.

"Who's asking?" Junie demanded from the doorway.

"NO! NO!" Hamp cried from his sleep, but no one heard him.

"He murdered my husband. I've come to kill him!"

"No, you ain't—"

The blast of the shotgun woke him up. He rolled out of the hammock, still so numb he didn't know where he was at. The Colt in his hand, he busted inside the back door. He could hear Junie giving orders. When he reached the back door, he could see her standing in the front one. She held the shotgun ready.

Loud protests in Spanish were telling her they would do nothing. "Don't shoot. Don't shoot."

"I'm here," he said to her. "What's happened?"

"She said she'd come to kill you."

He hugged her shoulder and at the same time

saw the woman in the green dress sprawled on the ground.

"I'm sorry, Junie."

"No need to be. I know how these feuds go. They have to end this way. Folks like her ain't got any better sense."

Hamp heard her. He spoke in Spanish to the men. He could tell Kathren Muldoone was dead; they all had their sombreros off and stood back from her.

"You can take her body. I'll get you a blanket."

The older one bobbed his head. "Gracias, señor."

She set the shotgun down and when he came past her, she asked, "It's finally all over, isn't it?"

"Yes, Junie, I sure hope it's over. Maybe now we can live our lives."

Epilogue

The union of Junie and Hamp Moser produced four living children. Hamp was killed in a horse-and-buggy wreck in 1902. Junie followed him in 1910. Their eldest, Hamp Junior, died in Cuba serving as a Rough Rider with Teddy Roosevelt. Milton, the middle boy, enlisted as dynamiter and machine gunner for Pancho Villa and was never heard of again. Their only daughter, May, married Ralph Bonham and they owned a successful Ford car dealership in San Antonio. Rex kept the B Bar M brand and the family ranch. His son, Hampton the third, used that iron until he lost the homeplace in a bank foreclosure during the Depression of the thirties. His son, Hampton the fourth, was a successful oil wildcatter and bought back most of the old place's acreage and built a magnificent three-story house at the headquarters. He still uses the brand on mixed cattle with ear.